TRUST AND TRIUMPH
Guardians of the Fae Realms: Book 15
JL Madore

Trust and Triumph: Guardians of the Fae Realms

JL Madore — 1st ed.

ISBN: 978-1-998372-72-0

CHAPTER ONE

Lark

Smoke and dust fill my lungs as I gasp for air, the taste of ash heavy on my tongue. My eyes burn as I blink, grit irritating them as I scan the scene of chaos. The once grand library of the Amberloq mountain retreat has been reduced to a smoldering wreck.

Books are scattered across the floor, pages torn free, singed and fluttering like burned leaves. The shattered remnants of shelves jut out at odd angles, threatening to impale anyone who comes too close.

I'm disoriented, lying among the wreckage, trying to piece together what happened. Jagged concrete is stabbing my wing and, by the wet warmth spreading down my hip, I'm pretty sure I'm bleeding.

It comes back to me in a blur at first and then rushes in with terrifying clarity. Shift and I were leaving the kids to help with the search for the Gen-3 infiltrators.

When the bomb went off, we were approaching the door to

the corridor. A deafening explosion detonated, and the power of the blast threw us off our feet and sent us flying.

"Shift?" I cough out his name and push up onto my elbow.

"Here." Shift's deep voice is strained but steady.

I find him in a push-up position, sprawled over River and Bay with a heap of wood and shelving lying across his back.

Scrambling on shaky legs, I stumble closer. "Shit. Are you all right?"

"It's not me. The boys are unconscious and if I move, I'm afraid they'll be crushed by the debris falling on them. They are much frailer than I am."

As quickly as I can, I grab the end of a piece of broken shelving and sling it off to the side. I take a few more minutes to dig them out and then I'm helping Shift to his feet.

"Are you all right?" I brush off his shirt, my adrenaline pumping as I take in his disheveled appearance. His golden hair is streaked with soot, and his clothes are singed and torn.

"I sustained minimal damage." Shift grunts, wincing as he straightens. "My system is functioning well within acceptable ranges. I am more concerned about you. Where is this blood coming from?"

"I'm not sure," I say, more worried about the angry red burns on his arms and the blood dripping from a gash on his forehead. "You need to heal yourself first."

"Already working on it. Now, let me see."

Without waiting for a response, he tugs my shirt up my ribs and my pants down my hip. There's no use arguing with him. He's a healer and one of my mates. There's no way he'll let me check on the others until he's sure I'm good first.

While he tends to my injury, I watch his wounds mend before my eyes. His hands are heaven as he channels his molecular realignment ability and knits me back together.

When he straightens, I breathe a sigh of relief. "Now the others."

He scans the room, his golden eyes filled with concern. "You find them, and I'll triage their status."

"Right." I pull my pants back up and bend to check on the two teenagers at our feet. River's marine blue feathers are battered and covered with drywall dust and debris, but I don't see any injuries.

Bay has a few minor cuts and scrapes marring his skin, but nothing that we need to worry about right now. "I think they're fine."

Shift seems to agree and moves toward the kids pinned against the window wall. "They are already regaining consciousness."

I spot a hand poking out from beneath a pile of broken wood. It turns my stomach to know that the kids I protected for two years in the goblin camp have been targeted by this level of violence when they are working on rebuilding.

I grip the edge of what looks like a broken shelf and lift with all my might. It doesn't even move.

"Shift. Help me with this debris."

Together, we unearth Warren, freeing him from confinement.

"Where is your damage?" Shift's hands move over Warren's arms and legs, assessing his injuries. When he brushes his sides, the young warrior winces. "You have sustained several breaks along your ribs. Lay still for a moment."

While Shift works on him, I continue to search.

River and Bay are both awake and sitting up now. "Once you feel up to it, help us find the others."

By the time Shift finishes healing Warren, we've found three more of the kids.

"Shift, hurry!" River shouts, pointing to Glen.

I get there first and the instant I see him, it's obvious he's dead. There's a chunk of wood spearing into the side of his neck and a pool of blood under his body. "Oh, damn it."

"It's bad right?" River says, reading my expression.

"Yeah, buddy. It's bad."

Shift rushes over and frowns. "I detect no life signs. I am sorry."

I swallow against the blockage at the base of my throat. "So am I. He was a great kid."

Bay sets a dusty blanket over Glen's upper body.

Each rescue after that brings a mix of relief and sadness. They deserve better from life than what they've gotten. These kids are in the prime of their lives and have already been through so much.

This is senseless.

With each rescued trainee, my concern for the structural safety of the library grows. Any moment could bring another explosion and another wave of debris crashing down on us.

"Okay, guys. I want to get us all up and out of here and secured in another part of the building that isn't about to collapse. Gather yourselves and get ready to move."

There's a general grumbling among the junior warriors, but they're strong kids and this isn't their first time dealing with violent tragedy.

"What about Glen?" River asks.

"I'll carry your friend," Shift says, bending to pick up his body.

River shakes his head. "No. Tactically, you're the strongest of all of us. You should be free in case we run into enemy Gen-3 soldiers."

"We'll carry him," Bay says.

As sad as it is that the kids have to deal with this, I'm proud of the way they're handling things. People show their true character in a crisis.

My thoughts stray to Flash, Mac, and Link. Where were they in the building when the explosion went off? What about our friends?

Ignoring the knot of fear twisting tight within my chest, I focus on what I know for certain.

We're not safe here and we need to move.

"Shift, do you hear anything from beyond the library?"

Everyone falls still.

As a bio-engineered super soldier, Shift's modified senses are one of our best assets.

I strain to listen. The air is filled with threatening creaks as dust crumbles and crashes to the debris-littered floor. Other than the settling of the building, I get nothing.

Shift's chiseled jaw flexes as he focuses. "I don't like it. This feels too quiet."

Quiet? That's certainly not how I would describe our situation. The library is a war zone, its walls twisted and charred, and its books reduced to useless ashes. But I see his point.

It's like there is an eerie stillness hanging heavy in the air... like a predator lurking just out of sight.

As the kids gather and prepare to move out, I study the group. They are battered but alert. "Everyone, be on guard. We don't know what's waiting for us outside this room."

I'm certainly no bomb expert, but it doesn't take one to see the gaping hole in the floor and know the detonation originated below us. Yet another reason we need to get down to the main floor and into another wing of the lodge where the kids can be safe.

Shift releases his wings and flies to the other side of the hole. "I'm going to assess the stability of the corridor. Stay together. If all is well, we'll move out."

Mac

The world swims into focus as I swipe the back of my wrist across my eyes. It does nothing to reduce the haze clouding my vision. My ears are ringing, too. And a thick layer of dust coats my tongue. Pushing myself up from the debris-strewn floor, I stagger and drop to one knee.

It takes a moment for the world to stop spinning and my surroundings to register. I was in the second-floor corridor of the sleeping quarters.

Dune, Flash, and I were searching for Gen-3 soldiers who infiltrated the Amberloq trials.

Seconds before the explosion rocked the building, I smelled the explosives and launched toward Dune to get him out of the line of fire.

That might've been the only thing that saved us.

The damage is incredible.

My chest tightens. Pain sears through my ribs, around my waist, and around to my back. My injuries make it hard to breathe, but they're not the only thing sucking the breath from my lungs...

I need to get to my mates.

Shift is a part of me. We are bound and my Sith cat needs to know he is well. Lark and Flash are special to me too. We haven't figured out exactly what we will be together, but there is something incredible happening between us.

Attraction. Loyalty. A promise of more...

And then there is Link. I'm not sure how he will fit into our couplings, but he is Shift's, so he is mine to protect as well.

My effort to get vertical works better the second time and I get my boots under me. With a push of will-power more than strength, I stand.

The air is thick with ash and smoke. It triggers a cough, and I groan as excruciating agony burns my chest. Doubled forward, I scowl at the scarlet mess splattering my palm. "Feckin' hell."

I hear Dune's voice through a warped tunnel of sound and turn to find the source.

My hearing is compromised.

He grips my arms at the elbows and steadies my stance. "You're hurt."

"I'll survive," I grit out between clenched teeth. A pool of blood gathers in my mouth, and I spit it out. Over two decades in the military, I've taken my share of hits. A few broken ribs and the possibility of a punctured lung don't even make the short list of the worst injuries I've sustained.

Distracted by my condition, I miss when Dune lists sideways. His wings come up in a hurry to counter his imbalance and I'm thankful because I'm not sure I could bear his weight if he needed me to catch him.

"How did you know to tackle me?" he asks.

"I smelled the explosives."

"All hail Sith cat senses."

I study him as he stands. "Are you steady?"

"As a newborn deer." With a pained smile, he grips my hand and straightens. "All right. We need to find the others. Where's Flash? He was with us when the world went to hell."

Dune and I spend the next few minutes searching through the wreckage. Nothing. No Flash.

There's no sign of him, but a massive section of the floor and ceiling is blown to fuck.

When I turn back to Dune, he's swiping his finger over the screen of his tactical watch. "Come on, Iceman. Let me know you and Lukas are all right."

I need to know that too. Lukas has been my friend and commanding officer for over a decade and he's in this clusterfuck situation somewhere.

I wait in silence, but we receive no answer.

Moaning in the distance brings our attention back to the most immediate problem at hand. "Help me with the trainees.

We need to assess the injured and move to a more secure section of the building."

Dune drops his hand and turns to survey what's left of the second floor. "I'll start at the far end and work my way to you."

He pushes off the floor and cuts through the air, flying over the chasm to the far end of the corridor.

"Flash!" I call out, my voice raw and hoarse. "Where are ye?"

Lifting my nose, I breathe deeply and call upon my Sith cat. It does little good. The air is thick with too many scents to pinpoint Flash, and my hearing is warbling in and out between a hollow nothingness and the scream of ringing.

Movement in a bedroom on my side of the devastation has me stumbling inside one of the trainee quarters. I find the mountain elf, Alryx-Ti sprawled on the floor, covered in plaster and debris.

It takes a moment to get over to him and I hesitate, wondering how the fuck I'll free him from the heap of obliterated construction materials.

Dune flies back to help. "Need a hand?"

"Aye, and a couple of ribs and a lung while yer in a givin' mood."

He passes an assessing gaze over me, and his brows tighten. "Fresh out, sorry, but I can help with this."

"Good enough."

The two of us work to free the elf. Dune does most of the heavy lifting, but I do what I'm able. I'm aware of the severity of my injury and there's no way I'm bleeding out up here when I don't know about my mates.

I'm going to find Shift, make sure he's alive and well, and then have him heal me so we can get out of this place and get on with our lives.

When Dune chucks the last piece of wallboard to the side, I help Alryx-Ti sit up. "Are ye whole, man?"

The massive elf tests his arms, wriggles his fingers, and brushes his hands down his body. "I think so."

"You're one lucky bastard," Dune chuckles, extending a hand to help him up. "Other than us, you were the closest to detonation. Glad you're not dead, my man."

"No more than me," he says, brushing himself off. The guy is a tank and has escaped virtually unscathed. "What can I do?"

I gesture to what's left of the corridor. "We're missing Flash for sure, but we don't know who else was in their rooms when the bomb went off. We're on search and rescue."

"But the Gen-3 soldiers who did this are still here," Dune adds. "So, we need to be quick about it and ready for attack."

I read his expression, watching for any sign that he might not be up for the task. There's nothing about the set of his shoulders or the emotions on his face that even hints at him being overwhelmed.

He was in the top position during the trials, and is continuing to prove himself now.

The acrid smell of burnt wood and scorched metal fills my senses as I scan the devastation. The explosion left the pristine corridor in ruins, with twisted metal and charred wood jettisoned through the walls of the sleeping quarters beyond.

The sight is gut-wrenching.

There will be dead.

"Mac! Over here," Alryx-Ti calls a moment later.

I rush over, my field training kicking in as I set to work, helping the young man he found down the hall. He's bleeding heavily from his arm, so I tear at the hem of my shirt to fashion a makeshift tourniquet.

The action of twisting to tear the fabric makes me see stars, but I refuse to pass out. With my world spinning, I hold out the fabric and realize I have no say in my state of unconsciousness.

I'm going to black the fuck out.

Well, shit.

CHAPTER TWO

Flash

I fly through the gaping hole in the floor to regroup with Mac and Dune just in time to see our russet-haired warrior collapsing. He's in freefall and about to impale himself on a jagged metal shard below him.

I pump my wings and close my arms around him in time to pull him to my chest and out of harm's way.

Dune's head snaps around and his eyes grow wide. "You're back."

"And my return seems well timed."

Dune arches a sandy brow. "It seems so."

I bend and lift an unconscious Mac, cradling him against my chest. "What are his injuries?"

"He said ribs and lung."

I let my eyes roll shut and seek Shift, probing the internal connection I share with my brothers-in-arms. *My brother, where are you? Are you well?*

His response comes back to me almost immediately. *Lark*

and I are about to lead the young warriors out of what's left of the library on the third floor. She and I are both well.

Stay there. I'm bringing Mac. He is injured. When I end the conversation with Shift, I update Dune, Alryx-Ti, and the two other trainees staggering down the hall to join us. "Shift and Lark are in the library on the third floor. I must take Mac there to be healed."

"We'll make our way and meet you there," Dune says. "Take Mac and get him fixed up."

Mac's eyes are already fluttering open, but I have no intention of putting him down. Mac is Shift's, and he is ours as well. We are a unit.

A family.

Pushing off the floor, I navigate the tangle of wires and exposed beams and take Mac to my brother.

The Gen-3 super soldiers infiltrated our ranks, posing as applicants. They attacked without warning.

Their objective: to weaken us from within.

For the moment, they have succeeded.

Shift is standing in the library's doorway when I fly through a hole in the floor. His golden eyes lock onto Mac in my arms. "What are his injuries?"

"Dune mentioned his ribs and lung."

As I'm assimilated into the chaos of the library, Lark and several of the young warriors are righting a large table. "Put him here so Shift can do his thing, sweetie," Lark says.

The relief that washes over me when I see her standing upright is incredible. Where Mac is Shift's, Lady Lark is mine.

My catalyst. My female. My lover.

My everything.

I set Mac on the table and step back as Shift assesses him. There is a great deal of violet bruising, and the skin along his side is almost completely black.

I step back to allow my brother space to work and extend a

hand for Lark to come to me. She moves without hesitation, her trust and affection a gift that still steals my breath every day.

"He'll be fine," she says, her words more of a whispered promise than a question.

"He will," I assure her.

Shift's primary enhancements are molecular alignment and healing. Mac couldn't be in better hands, and we all know it.

And while I marvel at my brother's abilities, I'm thankful for my own enhancements as well. Because standing here, with Lark pulled tight to my chest, I am blessed to be privy to her deepest emotions: her love and relief to have me here with her, her concern over Mac, her sadness over the loss of life, and most of all, her determination to stand strong and get the young ones somewhere safe.

My female is fierce.

"I cherish you, lovely lady," I whisper, brushing my lips across her temple. Moving a stray lock of ebony hair behind her ear, I lift her chin to meet her emerald gaze. "I sense no pain within you, but given the situation, I must ask. Are you well?"

"I'll be better once we ensure everyone's safe and we can get out of this death trap of a building."

I see the pain of loss in her glassy gaze and let that go. We will mourn the dead once the situation is resolved. I pull her tighter to my chest and stroke my hand over her silky black feathers.

Where my wings are retractable, hers are an ever-present feature of her beauty.

My ebony girl.

Mac's cat growls a moment before his eyes flutter open. "Ah, it's good to see yer face, mate."

Shift pauses his ministrations and folds over Mac's chest to press a kiss to his blood-stained lips. "It would be better if you weren't suffering."

Mac grunts. "Aye, I can't argue with ye there."

With the most pressing concern now resolved, I take in the room's devastation. Thank the powers of the universe Lark wasn't hurt—or, at least, wasn't hurt more seriously than Shift could heal—which I believe is more likely the case.

Books are strewn haphazardly across the floor, their pages torn and scattered. There is a group of injured trainees huddled together near a toppled bookcase. Their faces are pale and pinched, but they're alive. And if we have anything to do with it, they'll stay that way.

The crash and crunch of approaching footsteps echo up the hall. Lark and I break apart and take point, rushing to the entrance to the room as the first line of defense.

It might be Dune with Alryx-Ti and the others.

It's not.

But it's not Gen-3 soldiers either.

Lukas and Tundra burst into the room, their faces streaked with filth and etched with worry. "What's your situation?" Lukas asks, taking in the scene.

"One dead in here," Lark says. "Shift healed the rest of us."

"Two dead downstairs in the trainee quarters," Mac says, swinging his legs over the edge of the table to sit up. He runs a hand around the curve of his ribs and lets out a sigh. "I'm sure there would be more if we didn't have our genetically enhanced healer."

Shift dips his chin. "It is my honor to be of service. Although I wish my abilities were not needed."

Lukas nods. "You and me both."

"What about Link?" Mac asks. "Have either of you tried to contact him? It would help to know where he is and add his situational intel to ours."

"With everything that happened and rushing Mac up here to be healed, I haven't reached out," I admit.

"We shall do so now," Shift says.

The two of us focus on our brother-in-arms and reach out

across the private communication link we share. I sense Shift's presence immediately but...

"Link's neurosignal isn't online," Shift says.

"What does that mean?" Lark asks, searing me with a look of concern. "Is he unconscious?"

Shift frowns. "No. If he were merely unconscious, he should still register on our linked system as offline. I don't sense him at all."

Lark's panic increases as she meets my gaze. "Do you sense him?"

"No. I don't."

"Speaking of missing mates, where is Dune?" Tundra's question is deep with a growl, and I realize my omission in my assessment of our situation earlier.

"Apologies," I say. "Dune was well and organizing the survivors on the second floor when I left to bring Mac up to be healed. He intended to mobilize them and bring them up to join us."

"So, he isn't hurt?"

"No. Mac's Sith cat smelled the explosives and tackled Dune out of the path of detonation."

Lukas presses a clenched fist against his chest.

Whatever the gesture means, Mac waves away the praise and hops off the table. After testing his balance, he pushes off the table's edge and strides forward. "We need to secure the injured, find the rest of our people, and track down these fuckers. I, fer one, have had enough of this Gen-3 bullshit."

Tundra's snowy owl wings flare as he flexes. "What about Skye and Yarko? Has anyone seen them since this began?"

"Nothing so far, big guy," Lark says. "But I'm sure they're all right. They're both smart and Yarko is crazy protective of Skye."

He seems to consider that and moves on. "Are you all mobile and ready to move?"

Lark nods. "We are."

Lukas shares a look with Mac and if I didn't know better, I'd say they share telepathic communication like my brothers and I do. Perhaps it stems from them fighting as a unit for years, but they seem to convey something from one to another without speaking.

"All right, then. Let's move." At Lukas' command, everyone readies to leave.

Bodies shift toward the opening in the wall, and I slide my hand under the fall of Lark's wings and against the small of her back. "Stay close."

"Always," she grins. "How else will I save your perfect ass when things go wrong?"

I hear the teasing in her voice and chuckle. "I suppose that's true. I'm thankful to have you here to keep me safe."

~

Lark

I'm not sure how we ended up in this situation, but having Flash, Mac, and Shift here with me makes it almost bearable. What about Link? Reaching across the private communication channel I've shared with the boys since the first awakening of their heightened powers, I try myself.

Link? Are you there?

When nothing comes back to me, Shift meets my gaze. "There could be several reasons for the silence. The Gen-3 soldiers might've broken our communication, or perhaps he suffered a system error, or maybe they've taken him out of range. The three of us have never been separated and tried to communicate. It is possible."

These explanations don't make me feel any better.

With Lukas and Tundra leading the group, we fall into step and begin the evacuation of the third floor. I direct the kids, watching over my young warriors like I have for the past two years.

"Do you think the Gen-3 infiltrators are still here, or do you think they've bugged out?" River asks no one in particular.

"We need to assume they're still here," Lukas says. "So, no talking, and everyone stays liquid and lethal."

Liquid and lethal.

That's probably good advice. We have no way of knowing how many of the Amberloq applicants were genuinely here to join our military force. Likewise, we have no way of knowing how many moles were here to target us.

We make it to the wooden banister of the open staircase and meet up with Dune's group. There's a tender moment when Lukas, Tundra, and Dune exchange an embrace and then they're stepping apart.

"What do you know for sure?" Lukas asks.

Dune snaps right back to warrior mode. "This staircase doesn't seem to have suffered structural damage, but we've had to dodge more than one point of detonation. There were multiple bombs, and this entire wing of the lodge is more use to us as kindling than shelter."

Lukas frowns. "We need to secure the injured while we deal with the dangers. You two know the layout best. Scout ahead and find us a less damaged part of the building."

"We'll clear the path of obstacles and potential threats." Tundra grips the railing of the third-floor landing and drops into the empty space beyond, his wings flaring out with a span of white feathers.

"Don't get dead, friends." Dune flashes us a smile and then rolls over the banister, grinning as he falls after his mate.

Mac gestures for the kids to close the distance. "Stay tight together and move as quietly as ye can. Assume the enemy is close."

We move through the damaged halls, Lukas and Flash in

front, Shift and Mac at the back, and me in the middle of the pack, keeping a watchful eye on the injured. The explosions have knocked out the electricity and created a smoky haze in the air.

When we arrive on the first floor, a distant crash followed by shouts has us tensing.

Lukas frowns. "Mac, you and Flash check it out. Shift, Lark, and I will get everyone locked down."

"What about the rec room on the lower level?" I offer. "It's big enough for all of us and is at the end of the far wing. There might not be damage there."

"There's also a bar and a fridge," River says.

"And a lovely stone fireplace," Flash says, sending me a heated gaze.

Laughter bursts from me and my cheeks flush hot. The images of Flash, Shift, and I having sex against that stone fire-place are inappropriate and untimely.

And exactly what I needed to break the tension.

"Yes, and a fireplace," I repeat.

Thankfully, everyone is focused enough on our safety and our tasks not to pay much attention to my sudden embar-rassment.

"Heads on a swivel, everyone." Mac gives Shift a meaningful look before he and Flash disappear around the corner, leaving us to secure the injured.

I place a hand on Shift's arm and squeeze. "He'll be fine. He has his skills, and you have yours. Let's get everyone locked down."

Lukas winds around the stairway and continues down one more floor to the basement.

We make our way to the far wing of the lodge quickly and without incident. At the end of the hall, I'm relieved to find the recreation room untouched by the destruction of the day.

"Put the most severely injured of us on the couches," I say, pointing to the oversized furniture. "The rest of you relax on the carpet. River, grab any water or soda you find in the cooler fridge and hand them out. Bay, turn on the fireplace so we can get some heat and light in here."

While everyone settles in, Shift and I oversee the well-being of those who were hurt. He's healed several of them but hasn't had a chance to look over the trainees Dune rescued from the second-floor barracks.

Moment by moment, things settle down. The injured are lying on the oversized couches, the young trainees sink onto the floor lining the wall, and those of us who are well enough to stand and fight remain on our feet.

Like Mac said, we need to keep our heads on a swivel to be vigilant and ready for further attack.

CHAPTER THREE

Shift

*W*ith the injured secured and everyone healed, I try again to reach Link. The three of us have been connected through the magic of our system programming since we first came online. To not have a sense of him with me is incredibly disconcerting.

When nothing comes back to me, I move into the far corner of the room to run a systems analysis and try again. I won't stop until I find him.

If the situation was reversed, he'd never stop looking for me. Despite what people think, Link is worth it. There's no denying he can be difficult, inconsiderate of those he deems unworthy, and frustratingly self-involved—buy he's also our brother.

Flash and I know the male behind the programming.

He's not as tough and independent as he pretends to be. In fact, of the three of us, he's the most alone and afraid to be rejected.

When Brass and his scientists created us as genetically bio-engineered super soldiers, we were led to believe we were special and vital to the realm. Then, when our genetic enhancements didn't activate, we were deemed defective and put into stasis—for over a decade.

That is, until Lark and Mac changed everything.

Slipping behind the wall of the fireplace, I find a shadowed corner at the end of the bar and reach out across our internal communication channel once again. *Where are you, my brother?*

"Still nothing?" Lark whispers.

I open my eyes and find her standing before me, worry clouding her gaze. "He's not answering, and I can't sense him anywhere within our joint systems. Nothing like this has ever happened before."

Lark slides her arms around my back, and I pull her tight against my chest. The way her lush curves fit against my muscled frame is a pleasure, but when she presses her cheek against my shoulder and nuzzles her face against my neck, the comfort of it steals my breath.

She's incredible.

While we're still enjoying our embrace, Lukas strides over, staring at his tactical watch. "Shift, you're with me."

"Where are you going?" Lark asks, stepping back.

"To find Link," he says.

Lark looks from him to me and then back again. "How will you find him? Shift and Flash can't connect with him, and this place is not only massive but also a war zone."

"It's also crawling with Gen-3 soldiers," I add.

Lukas flips the face of his watch so we can see the blue dot in the center of the screen. "When it looked like Link might bolt, I had a track program added to his system."

"I'm not sure whether to be thankful or offended by that," I say.

Lukas shrugs. "It was a tactical decision when his loyalties were in question. I won't apologize for doing my duty."

"Nor should you have to," I say.

I'm not surprised Lukas put a tracking program on Link. I *am* surprised Link didn't realize it.

And he's not wrong.

More than once Link urged us to abandon our Amberloq duties and find ourselves a new home.

Flash and I refused to leave our mates.

"And you're sure he's here?" Lark asks.

"I am."

"But you don't know what shape he's in?"

Lukas taps his finger against the readout information. "I don't have vitals hooked up to the link, but if his brothers can't connect with him, I assume it's bad."

Lark doesn't hesitate to push me toward the door. "Go. Find him."

My feet remain firmly planted, unconvinced. "What if the Gen-3 soldiers find you?"

She lifts her chin and meets my gaze. "Between me, Alryx-Ti, River, Bay, and a dozen other warriors, we will put up one hell of a fight. Link needs you. I feel it. There's no way he'd be cut off from you for this long if he wasn't in trouble."

There isn't an ounce of doubt or fear in her, so I take her at her word. "Very well. Be fierce until I get back."

She winks. "Always."

After a quick brush of our lips, I leave my female and follow Lukas through the door and along the basement corridor. We exit out a set of sliding glass doors and I breathe fresh air for the first time in...

Has it truly only been thirty-seven minutes?

As baffling as that seems, my internal clock is functioning perfectly. Since the moment I woke on the floor of the library until now, less than forty minutes have passed.

"Stay close to the wall," Lukas says, his gun poised and pointed ahead as we race along the cast shadows of the building. "We don't know what heightened senses the Gen-3 soldiers possess, but hopefully, they aren't looking for us out here."

The two of us make good time, racing along the exterior of the lodge, following the tracking signal on Lukas' watch. When we turn the corner, my breath locks in my chest—

The entire side wall of the building has collapsed.

There's nothing but a gaping four-story hole, an enormous pile of stone rubble, and the twisted ends of floors and walls hanging unsupported in the open air.

"Fucking hell," Lukas says.

Agreed. That's about all you can say. "And Link is somewhere within this mess?"

"Twenty yards." Lukas points the way.

I search through the debris, the two of us stepping lightly and balancing on rubble, trying to scale the debris to find to my fallen brother.

There is no smoke like there was upstairs, but there is a lot of heat. I'm not sure what the cause of the roiling inferno is, but it doesn't truly matter. I would walk into the fires of a volcano a hundred times if it meant preserving the life of someone I love.

"He should be right here, somewhere," Lukas says, stopping just short of where he's pointing. "I'm worried we'll crush him if we go any further."

I calculate the stability of the materials underfoot and he's not wrong... at least if we were human. "Our framework can withstand eight point three times the compression a human body can. We may proceed without endangering his well-being."

Lukas swallows. "If you're sure."

"I am."

The two of us continue edging our way deeper into the field of debris.

Using my ocular enhancements to scan for the presence of

thermal targets does nothing to help us locate him. Everything is washed in an orange/red glow of heat from the explosions.

And then I see it.

The blond hair.

The mechanical connections of fiber and cabling dangling out from the bloody stump of a neck.

"He's been decapitated." My words come out hollow as my systems are overloaded with grief.

I am a healer...

I don't have the technical understanding of our creation to reconstruct my brother from a catastrophic injury such as this...

Especially not here...

I would need a laboratory... and schematics... and the tools Brass patented to create us...

Lukas is speaking, but my system is in such a state of flux, I'm not processing. He grabs my jaw and turns my face to meet his gaze. "Shift, listen to me, man. It's not Link. It's Alpha."

"Alpha?"

Lukas has turned over the severed head and found the body of my fallen friend. The first of our kind, genetic prototype Alpha-6, has been terminated past what I imagine is repairable damage.

My heart aches for the loss. "He was a good male who spent only a few days living life freely as an equal and a warrior of the realm."

"He deserved better," Lukas says.

"He did, but at least he died while living instead of being locked in stasis."

The two of us continue to sift through the rubble, silent and consumed in our thoughts. As sad as I am about Alpha, I am also pleased he passed as the warrior he was created to be.

"Here, Shift." Lukas has found another body and I recognize

the set of Link's shoulders the moment he uncovers him. "I think he's alive. Hurry! Help me get him free."

I rush to Link's aid.

The moment I touch him, I access his vitals. His systems are offline, and his synaptic function is weak. He's been rendered unconscious, but unlike Alpha, he remains intact.

Flash, we found Link. I convey over our shared communication channel. *He is offline and I have yet to determine his injuries.*

Where? Flash asks.

I relay our location as I assess Link's status, the loss of Alpha echoing through my programming.

And what of Beta?

Kneeling next to my fallen brother, I search past the deep gashes and dark bruises marring Link's skin. His once immaculate blond hair is matted with blood. He's taken damage, but nothing I find should have severed his system function.

What am I missing?

"Brother, can you hear me?" I ask, desperation clawing at my chest.

"Damn," Mac mutters, rushing to a stop after emerging through the opening in the lodge wall with Flash. "What can we do?"

"I need access to medical supplies and the schematics and equipment Brass and his science team used to maintain our systems."

"Are those things accessible here?" Mac asks.

Lukas meets his gaze. "No. The equipment and the schematics are back at Thornebane Castle with Josie and the Dornte science team."

"Then we open communications and get Shift the information he needs."

Lukas doesn't look convinced. "They gutted the communication room. Even if we make contact, that doesn't get Shift the equipment he needs."

No. It doesn't. "Then Flash and I will fly him back to the castle and work on him there."

Mac's russet hair brushes his shoulders as he shakes his head. "With Link in your arms, the two of you will be vulnerable and too easy to take out."

Lukas curses. "Then we'd be down three super soldiers in one day."

"Three?" Flash repeats. "Who is the third?"

"Alpha has been terminated," I say.

Flash stares at me in disbelief. "What about Beta?"

"We have yet to locate him."

Flash's attention drops to scan our surroundings. "If Link and Alpha are here, Beta is likely here too."

"I'll stay and search for Beta," Lukas says. "Mac and Shift, you take Link down to the basement. Tundra, escort Flash to the clinic. Dune, get a comm link up with the castle. Tell them what's going on and get Josie and the science team online to talk to Shift."

Tundra stiffens. "Tactically, if I were the attacking force, I would take out the clinic and anticipate us needing supplies."

Lukas meets his gaze. "Agreed, but there's nothing to be done about that. We lost Alpha. We don't know about Beta. We might have the ability to save Link."

"I should go to the clinic," I say, countering Lukas' assessment. "I'll have a better chance of determining what tools could be useful."

Lukas nods. "If you think that's best."

"I do."

Mac grips my hand tightly and I give him a reassuring squeeze. "Then off ye go. Dune and I will take Link downstairs and do what we can to stabilize him until ye get back."

～

Flash

As Shift and I follow Tundra through the corridors of the resort lodge, I can't shake the devastation of losing Alpha. How can he be dead? We're super soldiers. If one of us—built to be an indestructible weapon—can be killed, what chance do Lark, Mac, and the others have against the violence of Brass and his Gen-3 army?

I've been so consumed by the upside of love and creating bonds, I never considered the downside...

Losing that love.

I consider myself a powerful male, but could I survive the loss of Lark? No. I don't think I could.

My focus shifts to Link's situation and the possibility of losing him. He can't die. We need him. Shift and I are independent and can stand on our own, but Link has always been our guiding force.

He challenged us.

He tested our limits.

He held us together as a unit.

Losing him isn't an option.

"Almost there," Tundra murmurs, his voice barely audible. "Just around this next corner. On your toes."

As we round the last bend, my heart sinks. The clinic door is open, and the interior lies in tatters. We face debris and rubble and the same level of destruction we've encountered at every turn.

"I really hate these assholes," Tundra says.

"No more than we do," I add.

The enemy mercilessly ransacked the clinic and left nothing but chaos in their wake.

"We'll find what we need," Shift says, pegging me with a stern gaze. "If we have to make do to save him, then that's what we'll do. Understood?"

I nod. "Understood. Let's find what you can use and get back. I don't like being separated from them."

"Agreed."

With Tundra standing sentry at the clinic door, Shift and I sift through the wreckage. It's difficult to know what is still useful amidst the destruction, but I stack the tools I find strewn across the floor onto a metal tray for Shift to assess.

In the back of the refrigerated unit, there are still some vials that remain cool, so I put them in a cooler and snap some ice packs to lie over top of them.

As we scramble to salvage what we can from the destroyed clinic, I can't help but feel a sense of gnawing urgency. If we don't know what happened to Link or why his systems are offline... how will we know what to do to save him?

CHAPTER FOUR

Lark

$\mathcal{I}$ can't stand the helplessness consuming me as Shift works to stabilize Link. There's nothing I can do. Lukas is a magical marvel and Mac stepped up during the few moments when Shift needed an extra set of hands. But I don't offer any medical skills that can make this situation better.

"He'll be all right." Flash steps in behind me and lays his arms across my shoulders. "Whatever they did to him, Link's much too ornery to let them win."

"And arrogant," I add.

Flash's chest bounces with his silent amusement. "Yes, and arrogant."

I close my eyes, thankful for Flash's arms around me. It feels like he's the only thing holding me together. The day has worn me out and I want nothing more than to be done with the complete nightmare.

Flash uses his emotional enhancements to soothe me, easing my worst fears. He is my joy and my safe place. I haven't felt this kind of peace around other people since I was a kid.

My childhood wasn't easy, but there were periods of time when it didn't occur to me that it was hard. "When this is over, I'm going to take the four of you to the forested jungle where I grew up. Much of it was destroyed in the raids of the Usurper Queen, but some of my favorite places are still there."

"Something to look forward to. Tell me about it."

With my eyes closed, I let myself get lost in my memories. I tell Flash about growing up within the structure of the Elbirfae community, about how the elder females took me in when my parents died, and how I used to fly high in the canopy to lie on the top branches and watch the dappled sunlight peek through the leaves.

"It made you feel so safe," Flash says.

With his hands pressed against my bare skin, he's reading my emotions and feeling what I felt firsthand.

It's crazy. When he first did it, and I found out what he was doing, I was outraged and didn't want him touching me. Now, I find the sharing not only intimate, but bonding.

And with my eyes closed and his hands pressed against me, I forget for a moment why we're standing here. For this moment, I'm lost in the warmth of his touch and the safety of his arms.

With him, I can shut out the world and there is nothing but him and me... and my rapid pulse rate... and the ache between my thighs... and the solid cock pressed against the crease of my ass.

My eyes fly open as Flash's hand shifts from my shoulder to my mouth and I'm lifted off the floor. *Hush, lovely. Don't draw attention and no one will be the wiser.*

My mind is spinning, but I don't protest. I'm not doing Link or Shift any favors by hovering.

Flash moves us quickly and quietly into the pantry cupboard behind the bar and locks the door behind us. It's pitch dark, but he doesn't turn on the lights. *I need you, Lark. The fragile nature of mortality hit me this afternoon. It's shaken the foundation of what*

I thought I knew. Reassure me you are whole and safe and mine to love.

As his words whisper through my mind, his hands tug my shirt up my ribs and force my arms up so he can pull it over my head.

There's something desperate in his voice and I don't have any intention of turning him away.

What if someone comes looking for us?

He's already unfastening the front of my pants and shoving the fabric down my thighs. *If they dare to interrupt, they're in for quite a show.*

He lifts one foot, removes my boot, and then the other. Once my feet are free, he pulls my underwear down, spreads my legs, and drops to a knee before me.

A rush of emotional charge sweeps over my skin, heightening my sensations. He's hungry, but more than that, he needs this.

He needs *me.*

His mouth on my core has me gasping, and he chuckles into my mind. *Hush now, lovely. Or maybe you want to bring someone else in? I know how you like to be shared.*

I sink my fingers into his hair and drop my head back as he swings my knee over his shoulder. His tongue delves without apology, taking what he needs.

With no light in the dark space, my senses are heightened, driving me higher.

He's not wrong. I didn't know how erotic it could be to be shared, but now is not the time.

He runs his palm up my chest and stops to thumb over my nipple. *I'll never get enough of this. If our lives were simpler, I would dedicate my days to making you come into my mouth.*

I press my lips together, swallowing the groan that tears from my throat. Heat spreads through me, filling my chest and building low in my belly.

I'm lost to him.

As his one hand tweaks my nipple, his other moves to my clit and starts a torturous rub. Another rush of heat sweeps through me and he growls against my flesh. *Yes. I want your cream in my mouth. I want to feel you, taste you, hear you cry out across our bond. We are alive and together at this moment. You are mine.*

Flash, my sweet and curious lover, has grown bold and confident. And somewhere along the line, he discovered dirty talk. It's sexy and I love it.

I love *him*.

My arms bristle with goosebumps as he teases me. In the quiet darkness, it's so easy to sink into the bliss of him cherishing me.

"I love you," I whisper into the darkness. "I love you, Flash."

He stands, lifting me against his chest as his cock notches at my wet core.

"I love you," he repeats, kissing my shoulder, the line of my throat, and finally, my mouth. His lips claim mine, the salty tang of my core coating his tongue. "I love you with everything I am and will ever be. I am yours. Don't ever leave me."

The desperation in his plea is raw. He doesn't mean me walking away from him. He means me being taken from him in death.

"I will claw my way back from the afterlife to stay with you. Forever and always."

Flash thrusts his hips and his cock slides in deep. His bio-engineered strength cages me in his arms and, with my heels locked around the backs of his thighs, I arch back to improve the angle and take him deeper.

I gasp as he rocks into me.

Our bodies crash together, his arms encircling my ribs as my hands grip his shoulders, my fingers digging into the hard muscle. He groans, the ferocity of our passion unlocking a primal need to consume one another.

Spinning away from the shelves, he pins me against the stone wall beside the door and shifts his grip to hold me by my thighs.

I claim his mouth in a rough, lust-fueled kiss, gripping his shoulders with bruising force as he picks up his rhythm.

The sensations wash over me.

The frantic friction of rough thrusts in and out. The pinch of his grip on my flesh. Our breathy pants building as my orgasm takes hold and his hips rock.

It's all too much—

I ignite, my body spiraling behind a rushing wave of throbbing bliss. My pussy clenches tight around him and my orgasm catches fire.

The pleasure spreads wild and fast through my core, shattering me far beyond the physical.

Flash is my soul.

With his hand cupped over my mouth, he catches my throaty cries. And then he follows. His release hits in a wild rush, his shoulders going stiff as his hips thrust forward and lock.

How can I feel this good?

When our orgasms fade, Flash melts against me and a ragged breath tears from his chest.

My everything.

His words brush my mind with a gentleness that makes me wonder if he meant to speak them into our bond. This man claims more of me with every word, look, and gesture.

He's my everything, too.

He presses a kiss against my cheek and then eases out of me. The emptiness that follows is acute, and I wish we were back in our suite and the world wasn't pressing in on us.

"Pretend I'm cleaning you up properly as you deserve," he whispers, bending to slide my underwear up my legs. "Imagine me taking time to worship you and take care of my most precious treasure."

I smile in the darkness as he kneels a second time and pulls my pants up. "Although I like the idea of you facing the harshness of the world with a part of me inside you."

"Maybe your release will give me super soldier strength and stamina."

He chuckles and kisses my bare collarbone, offering me the ball of fabric that is my shirt. "If it does, I will make it my life's mission to keep you sexed and strong."

"I think you should."

The two of us finish putting ourselves back together, and then Flash takes my hand and unlatches the lock on the door. The soft, metallic *click* is followed by a slice of illumination from the hall, and I wince at the intrusion of light into our stolen moment.

Flash leads the way out toward the bar area of the recreation room and stops short just outside the door. "Connor Mac? Is everything all right?"

Mac

Flash and Lark come sneaking out from the storage room behind the bar and I can't help but smile. It's amazing what a sexual release can do. After finding Link and losing Alpha, Flash had a haunted look of desperation that isn't there anymore.

Lark looks better too... other than her shirt being on inside out.

"Connor Mac? Is everything all right?" Flash asks, straightening to his full height.

"Dune reestablished the security feeds and is searching for

the Gen-3 soldiers. I came to see if ye want to join the offensive team."

"Finally," Lark breathes. "Something to do."

I understand her frustration. Warriors thrive when there is someone to fight or fires to put out. We don't do well waiting around while others do the saving.

"I will get your battle vest and our weapons," Flash says, striding off.

Lark meets my gaze and blushes. "How long were you standing there, waiting?"

I lift a shoulder. "Don't worry about that, lass. Whatever the two of ye shared, our boy needed it. He looked hollowed out earlier. Now he's ready to get out there and fight the enemy."

She blinks at me. "But this certainly wasn't the time or the place. I feel bad."

"Well, don't." I step closer and drop my mouth to her ear, so our conversation doesn't carry. "Soldierin' is hard, lass. It's hard, and it's ugly and it takes a lot from us. If ye can turn that adrenaline and emotion into pleasure, even fer a moment, then ye do what ye need to do. We've all been there: me, Lukas, Tundra, Dune, and every soldier on my squad."

She searches my gaze, the worry clouding her amazing emerald eyes clearing as my words sink in. "Thanks, Mac. I don't want to let anyone down. Honor went out on a limb, naming me as an Amberloq General. I want to earn the respect that comes with the title."

I'm standing too close—I know this.

Except my cat is prowling at the forefront and the scent of sex on her skin is too tempting to step away. "Ye know that bit I just said about stealin' a moment of pleasure, even when it's not the time or the place?"

She eases her head back and swallows. "Yes."

"Well, ye smell like sex and the sound of yer throes of release bein' stifled behind the door has me wantin' to steal a little pleasure myself."

"I thought we were meeting Dune and the others."

"Och, we are. I just meant a little nuzzle before we're off. If ye don't object, I mean. The lines between us haven't been drawn... If I'm out of line—"

"You're not." She steps closer and wraps her arms around me in an embrace. "I don't object. I'm not sure what we are or will be, but you and I started down this road together and we'll figure it out together. What do you need?"

Running my hands up the back of her shirt, I pull her against me and claim her mouth. Lark's lips are velvety soft and yet her kiss is firm.

This.

This is all I need to calm my cat and to throw myself back into the line of fire. Just a moment of warmth and affection shared between two attractive people who care for one another.

I think it's more than that, but we haven't had time to let things breathe, so I don't want to assume.

The kiss ends much too quickly.

I ease back, a little breathless, and am pleased to see she's in the same state. "The world awaits."

"Yeah, it does," she breathes.

Flash is standing behind Lark, his brow arched as he watches us together. "I liked that," he says.

"Not half as much as I did." I swallow and brush my fingers over my lips. "Thanks fer the moment, little bird. Perhaps we can circle back around to figurin' things out once the battle is won."

Lark traps her bottom lip between her teeth. "We'll make a point of it."

Flash lifts her weapon's vest over her head and secures the straps around her sides. "Dune is back and is showing Lukas and Tundra something on his tablet."

I wink at Lark and then drop back into my soldiering role. "Then let's go see what he found."

~

Shift

As my hands skim over Link's body, I try everything I know and can think of to reestablish his connection with our system functions. The three of us have been linked since our creation. To not be able to sense him is terrifying.

"He seems to be stabilizing," Lukas says, his magical healing pulsing under my palms. "Are you getting anything from his diagnostic systems?"

"No. If I didn't know he was genetically enhanced, I would never guess it based on assessing him now."

Lukas frowns. "It's fine. For now, we save his life. Once he's out of danger, we work on the disconnect of his system from yours."

That makes sense.

Alive is better than not. We can work from there.

"Hey, fellas," Mac says, ducking his head behind the stand up screens the kids found to give me and my patients a little privacy. "How are things here?"

"As good as can be achieved, given the fucking mess we're stuck in." The acidic venom in my words has me gripping the edge of the table and drawing a steadying breath. "Apologies. I didn't mean to take my frustrations out on you."

Mac strides over and cups my cheek in his palm. "Ye needn't apologize to me, soldier boy. I understand exactly what this day has taken out of ye. If it makes ye feel any better, we're headed out to get some justice."

Lukas steps away from the table, looking pale and almost as

exhausted as I feel. "Oh, yeah? I could use a bit of justice. What's up?"

"Dune resurrected the security feed. He located four Gen-3 soldiers scaling down the jagged rock face toward a waiting Humvee. The winged warriors are heading down to intercept."

I do the math in my head. Dune, Tundra, Lark, and Flash have the capability of flight. Link is down, Alpha is dead, and Beta is still unaccounted for. "Four on four is not enough when only Flash is matched to their strengths. I should help."

"Not on yer life," Mac says. "Yer spent and are benched until yer systems replenish."

"But they need more force if they are to come out of this whole and victorious."

Mac won't hear it. He shakes his head and leans in so we're standing nose to nose. "Yer benched, mate. Yer in no shape to fight and I'll tie ye up and hold ye down myself if it comes to it."

I tilt my head, considering his words. "I'm not sure whether to be angry or aroused by that."

"Yer too fuckin' cute." Mac chuckles and eases back. "The point is, River, Bay, and several of the other Elbirfae trainees are going as backup. They'll be fine."

Lukas' brow pinches. "Have the kids take out the Humvee while the others go for the Gen-3. Then, no matter what happens, those assholes will remain as trapped as we are."

"The trainees aren't ready," I say.

Mac laces his fingers with mine and squeezes my hand. "They're angry and determined. They've also got skills. Besides, two-to-one odds in our favor should keep them safe enough."

Lark steps into our private area next. She takes in Link and then meets my gaze. "How is he?"

"Stable for the moment," I say, reminding myself that's better than where we were an hour ago. "We'll know more when we can get him to Thornebane Castle, and I have access to Brass' research."

She strides over to the table and leans down to whisper something in Link's ear. When she straightens, she smiles at me. "It won't be long now, sweetie. Dune got through to Rhylan at the castle. Help is on the way."

CHAPTER FIVE

Flash

"There—four Gen-3s making a run for it. East side of the mountain." Dune points down the slope of the jagged rock face, highlighting four soldiers who, until this morning, had been trainees here for the Amberloq trials.

My blood flares with the fire of adrenaline, the damage they've inflicted on my family and friends acting as the fuel to fan the flames higher.

We may have been in the middle of picking through the wreckage of their bomb strike, but no way in hell are we letting them get away.

"For Alpha," Lark says beside me, the same fire burning hot in her eyes.

"For Alpha," Dune and Tundra repeat, the massive Elbirfae warriors pitching themselves off the cliff edge, both with wings fully extended.

I release my own wings, my feathers catching the last rays of the fading sun. With a powerful thrust, I launch myself into the air, following in the wake of my comrades.

Lark is right on my tail, her ebony wings a stark contrast against the iridescent color of twilight.

In a streamlined plummet, we weave through the jagged crags and stoney peaks, closing the distance between us and the soldiers who follow my traitorous maker—Andras Brass.

Below, the Gen-3 soldiers scramble down the slope with the surefooted grace of mountain goats. Below them even further sits a Humvee waiting on a plateau halfway to the base of the mountain.

Do they honestly believe they get to attack us and then slip away under the cover of darkness?

No way.

Their sights might be set on escape, but ours are set on justice.

Lark and I split off, taking opposite flanks. Dune and Tundra continue straight on, creating a pincer movement. The soldiers might be Gen-3s, with enhanced reflexes and strength, but we have flight on our side.

Where my brothers and I were *constructed*, our entire creation engineered to perform the duties of the Amberloq, the Gen-3 soldiers were *modified* from beings of the realm.

If they weren't a member of a flying race before their transitions into being super soldiers, then they don't have the ability to fly now.

Greed and the need to mass produce made Brass careless and stupid.

The mountain that hampers their escape offers us a playground of tactical advantages.

I swoop in, my wings slicing through the air, feet striking out to collide with the first soldier. The impact jars me, but the soldier stumbles. His descent is halted as he scrambles to find a foothold.

I feel the satisfying crunch of bone as my fist connects with his jaw, then I'm back in the air, leaving him disoriented on the steep incline.

Lark engages her target with a swift precision that leaves me in awe. Even as new as she is to combat fighting, she trades blows like a warrior, graceful in a lethal dance of strength and agility.

Pride and admiration warm my chest.

Arousal stiffens my cock.

My female is fierce. Even knowing her foe has been enhanced to be physically and tactically superior to her, she fights with confidence and fire.

Dune and Tundra have engaged the other two, their own battles raging against the rugged backdrop of the mountainside.

Dune is brutal and relentless and uses the dangerous mountain terrain to assist him. Even as his opponent grabs a handhold and turns to fire lasers from his eyes, Dune laughs, shields himself with his wing, and launches a chunk of broken stone like a spear.

Tundra is a fluid force. He is strength and grace personified. He adapts and changes to navigate attacks like water racing down rapids. His snowy white wings not only act as transportation and shields, but are also incredible weapons.

Even as his opponent strikes out and tries to eviscerate him with mechanically enhanced talons, he dodges the strikes and deals damaging blows.

Before all this, I thought I understood what it meant to be a super soldier.

I was wrong.

Super doesn't come with genetic enhancement and bio-engineered strength. Super comes from the warrior's heart. It's about determination, bravery, and conviction to do what's right and hold the line even when outmatched.

The Amberloq Biome Generals are truly super soldiers.

That isn't to say that the four Gen-3 soldiers will be easy to beat. They won't. The only thing keeping them from thoroughly kicking our asses is their inability to meet us on a level playing field.

We can fly.

They can't.

And as Lukas would say—It sucks to be them.

My opponent is an Aswang with several rows of jagged teeth and long, curved claws like deadly sickles at the end of his fingers.

His fangs are dripping and as I battle, the stats of his race are flashing red on my ocular screen in my line of vision.

Aswang venom contains a paralytic agent.

Good to know. I don't intend to get bitten and fall to my destruction. No thanks.

The battle rages on as a symphony of strength and strategy, each of us playing our part. Grunts and groans echo around us, the sounds of combat bouncing off the hard surfaces of the mountain.

A shrill cry has me spinning to see Lark toppling backward in the air. Her opponent is a Hexenbiest and has used his powers of telekinesis to summon a cyclone of stone to bombard Lark.

Releasing my hold on the warrior I'm fighting, I cut through the champaign sky to help her. I check the distance of our two opponents from the vehicle below and curse. Lark didn't want the kids to engage if they didn't have to, but either they take out the Humvee or we won't be able to contain them.

"River! Mobilize your team and descend!"

"Affirmative," River shouts.

"Woo-fucking-hoo!" one of the others adds.

As half a dozen Elbirfae teens bolt over the crest of the cliff above, I return my focus to Lark and her opponent. In an ordinary battle, I know she could hold her own and even come out on top.

Against a genetically enhanced Hexenbiest super soldier... I won't take that chance.

She is mine.

Mine to love and mine to protect.

Lark

I flare my wings to slow the head over heels cartwheeling through the air and try to orient myself. The world is spinning and when you add with the adrenaline of a one-on-one fight with a Gen-3 surging through me, I might barf.

"Lark, shake it off, lovely," Flash shouts, his wings swept back and in full dive. He reaches me a moment later and stops with a speed and grace I know I didn't have when I was toppling. "Are you well?"

I shake off the last of the spinning and focus on the warmth of his gaze and the firm reassurance of his hold on my arms. "Better now. Thanks."

He studies me a moment more and then nods. "Then let's go win this fight."

When he launches off toward the Mount Hekko slope once again, I get back in the game and follow.

Instead of going back to his opponent, Flash seems determined to fight at my side to defeat mine. I hate feeling like I'm not holding my own, but then again, they are super soldiers and I'm not.

No matter how determined I am, Flash is more equipped to take on this enemy.

A guttural scream to my right has my head turning. My heart lurches as one of the Gen-3 soldiers falls, flailing in the open air around him.

He almost hits Storm as the kids descend to the Humvee, but

thankfully, the Gen-3's terrified cry is enough to warn the kids of the incoming threat.

The plummet of our enemy ends with a horrifying crunch, and then the scream abruptly cuts off.

Dune's opponent hangs impaled on the spike of a jagged stone outcrop.

As gruesome as his death is, after seeing Alpha's head severed from his body, I don't have space in my heart for remorse for them.

We *will* win this fight. For Link. For our comrades. For justice. It's a promise etched in every strike we make and in every gust of wind beneath our pumping wings.

"Fire in the hole!" River shouts from below.

The teens scatter into the air like a flock of startled moths, their wings pumping to get them clear of the impending explosion.

Boom!

The power of the detonation lifts the tires of the vehicle off the ground and sends a billowing cloud of flame and smoke into the air.

Debris and flames hurtle through the air and with it, the eradication of any hope of escape for Brass' Gen-3 soldiers.

With the Humvee dealt with, the kids hover in the air close by, hoping to act as our reinforcements.

River swoops in to assist Dune.

Tundra has Bay and Zephyr waiting in the wings.

And Ash is right there with Flash, hoping to get a shot to fight the enemy. Not that the enemy has much left in them.

Brass gave up on my guys for brighter, shinier possibilities. Big mistake. But it is a mistake that works in the favor of the good guys.

That's karma, baby.

I turn my attention to the male impaled below.

Is he dead or simply offline?

I drop toward the plateau to investigate when the rhythmic hum of helicopter rotors vibrates off the sheer mountainside. Twisting toward the sound, I find a silver speck on the horizon, glimmering in the light of the Dornte twin moons.

"Reinforcements are here," I call to the group. "Oh, and boys, you're in for a treat."

The kids look around, their curiosity morphing into amazement as Rhylan's dragon roars into the fray.

King Creed's mate creates an impressive silhouette in the moonlight. The beast is a force of nature, his scales shimmering as he swoops low, his hot breath gusting over us.

He's an intimidating sight, even for those of us who have seen his shifted form before.

And beside Rhylan's dragon, Princess Honor's figure stands out, her black and turquoise wings unfurled. She's a vision of power and grace, her long silver hair whipping in the wind, a stark contrast to the dark scales of the dragon beside her.

As Rhylan and the rest of the rescue party join us, the tide of battle shifts decisively in our favor.

The dragon darts in and grabs two of the Gen-3 soldiers in the vice grip of his talons. Then he rises to the compound grounds above and lands with a heavy thud. The pumping of his wings sends a gust of wind that stirs the dust around us and we raise a wing to shield our faces.

Princess Honor, never one to shrink from battle, joins me on the front lines.

"It's good to see you, Princess," I say.

She scans the scene, and frowns at the male impaled below us. "Although it seems we missed most of the excitement. What's your status? Dune couldn't tell us much beyond the fact that you'd been infiltrated and attacked."

"It's a long, sad story. We've got dead, missing, and injured. And I'm afraid your beautiful mountain retreat will probably need to be torn down."

She waves away my words and gestures for me to join her in climbing to the compound above.

Flash and Tundra secure the last soldier while Dune flies down to gather his opponent off the spike of stone.

When Honor and I land among the warriors, onlookers, and rescue crew, relief washes over me like a tangible thing. We fought, and we won.

We took down four more Gen-3 soldiers sent here to take us out. They may have caught us by surprise and started the fight, but we finished it.

I hope Alpha can rest in peace knowing we kicked their asses and they will be held accountable.

CHAPTER SIX

Link

$\mathcal{M}$y primary systems come online in scattered spurts, powering up enough to give me a glimpse of what's happened and then failing to reboot and plummeting me back into the darkness of stasis.

I despise stasis.

If there is a life-sucking purgatory where bio-engineered soldiers go to be tormented, it's stasis.

Neither here nor there.

Neither alive nor dead.

Just... stuck.

The memory gaps are frustrating. The darkness I'm locked in is haunting. But what really has my blood running cold in my veins is not being able to feel the connection to my brothers.

Brass and his scientists thought they had flipped our switches and simply turned us off. They hadn't. For more than a decade, we were aware—paralyzed and unable to communicate, but aware.

The loneliness of that mental isolation was only lessened by Flash and Shift... and more distantly, Alpha and Beta.

They kept me company throughout it all... a distant brush against my synapse... a probe into my thoughts...

And now that's gone.

Shift? Flash? Are you there?

They're not.

My primary enhancements make me a communication specialist. I host the private conversation channels between my brothers and—since the moment I first encountered her, and our enhancements activated—with Lark as well.

Lark? Are you there?

But no one is with me. For the first time since my creation, I am truly alone. Lying here, I try to access my motor functions, but none of my systems are responding properly.

What happened to me? Am I dead?

Accessing my memory files, I replay the data clips of the last moments recorded.

The Gen-3 soldiers seized Alpha... Beta and I took chase... there was a battle... they decapitated Alpha... there was an explosion...

I shut off the data access, but it does nothing to lessen the images of my fallen brother.

Alpha was terminated.

I despise Brass and his ambitions with everything in me. His dismissal of me and my brothers, his connections with the greedy and the vile, his decision to monetize the third generation of his creations for personal gain.

We were created to protect the Realm of Dornte.

We were meant to serve the Thornebane family and their reign.

We were supposed to be heroes.

No one thinks we're heroes now.

Well, maybe apart from our catalyst. Lady Lark has seen

through the judgement and opinions from the start. She stood by us and stood up for us. She advocated for our freedom to join the warriors of the realm. She's even grown to love us.

Well, maybe not all of us.

Flash, certainly. Shift, likely. Me...?

Part of me finds it alarming that she welcomed us with such acceptance. She's not one of us. How can she understand what we are and what they made us?

At first, I thought she was lying, but Flash touches her and would sense her deceit if she were.

And she's behind my walls. She communicates within our private channels. She sees and feels things within us we would never show others.

By now, she could've exploited her knowledge and turned it against us. Instead, she's forged intimate relationships with Flash and Shift and even invited me to join them.

I admit she is a delight I crave—I simply don't trust what it means.

When she's with me, my programming is scrambled. I am not myself. I am more irritable, more defensive, more obstinate.

And yet, she still claims to care for me.

Why?

There have been times, while I've been trapped in this darkness since the explosion, when I feel her touch. I hear the soft cadence of her voice. I smell the feminine essence that is uniquely hers.

I breathe deep and my body responds unbidden. She's either here or she's been here recently.

That shouldn't comfort me as much as it does.

I'm not needy like Flash or soft-hearted like Shift. I don't swoon over females or need them to cling to me to make me feel strong.

I live for my brothers—independently, but for them. We are a unit.

The gentle stroke of fingers against my cheek brings my sensory functions back online.

She's here.

Lark

"Don't you give up on us, Link. Your brothers need you to come back from this. I need you too. You are a fighter, so fight. Show us what you're really made of and open your eyes."

I straighten the sheet across Link's chest and squeeze his arm as I leave him to recuperate. For a moment there, I could've sworn I felt him with me.

I tread lightly, leaving Link's side, drawing the door closed behind me all but a crack. If he wakes up, I want him to feel welcome to join us.

Stepping into the living area, I find the boys engaged in a raucous game of cards. Mac is holding court at the center of the action, his hazel eyes gleaming with amusement. "Think ye have me on this one too, do ye?"

Shift waggles his brow. He looks hilarious in a backward baseball cap and tinted sunglasses. He accessed online images of poker players and is playing the part. "I've got your number, puss."

Mac snorts. "Puss, is it?"

Flash takes a long swallow of his drink.

They're on the second bottle of haze and that is impressive. Haze is a burgundy liquor favored by the realm for its fruity flavor, but it's strong and has taken down more than its fair share of big, tough men.

I stop on the periphery of their game, not wanting to disturb their fun. Mac slaps a card on the table. "Jack of diamonds, soldier boy. Things are getting interesting."

Shift laughs. "For us, maybe. I still have my pants. You're the one down to one sock and boxers."

Mac chuckles. "All part of my plan, boys. I'm lulling ye into a false sense of security."

Flash tips back his drink and sets the empty glass on the table. My playful super soldier has been cheered up with the evening's antics. The harsh realities of losing Alpha and almost losing Link are still raw but forgotten... at least for the moment. "Let's do this, Red. I'm in."

Mac grins. "That's the spirit, lad. We've got jacks over nines on the table and a possible flush."

"I'll pay to play." Flash's caramel eyes are bright and full of life. He tosses in the chips to match the raise and turns to Shift. "What about you, my brother? Would you like to take part in me stripping your mate naked?"

Ever the contemplative one, Shift regards his hand, his gaze flicking between his cards and the pile of chips in the middle of the table. He takes a gulp from his drink and gives Mac a sidelong glance. "While I will always be eager to strip you naked, I don't believe I'm needed. Carry on, Flash. He's all yours."

"So sure of yerselves, are ye, boys?" Mac teases.

Flash chuckles. "We know you're bluffing, puss. The statistical possibility that you have the cards to beat me is—"

Mac raises a hand and waggles his finger. "Hey, now. None of that. Ye might well be bio-engineered supercomputers, but it's bad form to calculate the odds while the play is ongoing. Poker is a game of instinct."

Stepping in behind Flash, I sneak a peek at his cards and hide my smile. Grabbing the bottle of haze, I top him up so I can share.

The punch haze gives off is more than fruity delight. It's practically magical. It's smoothed the rough edges of the past week and gives us exactly what we need—a night of flirty fun.

The tension of the past few days has been tough. Alpha's

loss. Beta, Skye, and Yarko still missing. And Link lying uncon-scious and disconnected from the internal communication system he shares with us.

But now that we're back at Amberloq Hall and the royal scientists, Doc, and Josie have all assured us Link has stabilized and is simply regenerating, it's time to unwind.

"Enough with the bravado, Mac," Flash says. "Show us what you've got."

Mac's cat lets off a long, sexy growl. "Do ye mean what cards I have or somethin' else, blondie? Cause either way, I'll rise to the occasion. And when I say I'll rise..."

He runs a suggestive hand over the front of his boxers, and I laugh and take another drink. "Oh, I'm sure they're very well aware of the double entendre."

Mac waggles his brows and combs his fingers over his scalp and through his long russet waves. "Well good, then. I'm not really the subtle kind."

No, he's not. He's direct and lets us know exactly what he wants and is thinking. It's one of the things I love most about him.

The guys too. They don't understand sarcasm or passive aggressive comments. Direct is best and Mac is a great fit that way.

He's a great fit in a lot of ways.

"All right, let's get this done," he says, bringing everyone's attention back to the game at hand. "Flash called. Shift folded. Now is the moment of truth."

"Now is the moment you lose your boxers," Flash says, grinning.

"Yer quite focused on getting' me naked, blondie. If ye got somethin' on yer mind, ye needn't go through the trouble of playin' cards to get it. We could toss the cards right now and move on to a more physical game."

Flash laughs. "Not on your life. You know I'm about to beat you and you're trying to seduce me into tossing my cards. I'll win those boxers and *then* we'll move to something more physical."

"Well now. It seems ye think yer in a win-win situation."

Flash's grin grows wider. "Seems so."

I laugh, taking another swig of fruity intoxication. Their camaraderie is infectious. It's grown so naturally over the past weeks. Sure, it's new, but I know to the marrow of my bones, it could be like this all the time.

We could be a family.

We just need Link to wake up and get on board.

Mac sets his cards on the table and fans them out for the others to see. "Read 'em and weep, boys. Four of a kind."

"Oh, that's a nice-looking hand, lover," Shift says, grinning. "But if I were a betting man—which tonight, I am—I'd say that knowing what's in my hand, there's a seventy-two percent chance Flash has a flush."

Mac's glee dissolves, and he pegs Flash with a look. "Tell me it ain't so. Ye wouldn't disrespect my lovely hooks by beating me on the river with a diamond, would ye, blondie?"

Flash laughs and sets down the ace and nine of diamonds. "I think I would. And while I'm at it, I think you owe me those boxers."

Mac arches a brow. "What if I'm not ready to surrender them yet? I still have a sock."

Flash waves that away. "I have no interest in your smelly old sock. I want the boxers. Come on, squad leader, show us what you've got."

I burst out laughing, as the moment grows increasingly lively and less focused on cards. Mac stands, hooks his thumbs into the waistband of his boxers and turns to give us his back. Then, in a move both swift and graceful, he pulls them down and bends to the floor, mooning us quite spectacularly.

I burst out laughing as the jaws of both Flash and Shift drop to the floor.

The men are on their feet in an instant and then Mac steps out of the black fabric and he straightens to face Flash. "A gentleman never squelches on a bet. Well played, blondie."

Flash's grin is back, and he accepts his bounty.

"Now, to yer seats, boys." Mac grins at me from across the table, his eyes full of fire and mirth. "I've still got a sock, so the game isn't over yet."

"Oh, it's over," Shift says, chuckling. "All you've done is encourage us to take you out so we can move on to the next round of fun."

Mac grins. "Ah, then my evil plan is working."

I love his evil plan. Mac is exactly what this crazy unit of bonding needs. He draws the boys out of their cerebral states. I have no doubt that, given time, he'll wear Link down too.

One day soon, Mac will have Link down to his last sock and flashing us all his bare ass.

And honestly, I'm looking forward to it more than I thought I would.

CHAPTER SEVEN

Mac

*W*aking from a deep sleep, I rub my eyes and shuffle towards the bathroom. Damn, Lark wasn't kidding when she warned me about haze. That stuff is lethal. Shift, Flash, and I got into it good, and the night passed me by in a blur of drunken delights. Wow. It's been a decade since I woke with blackout gaps.

I scrub my palm over my face and walk through the main part of the bathroom to the little toilet room off to the side. I leave the lights off for two reasons.

First, I'm in no shape to have illumination and I see well enough with my Sith senses.

Second, if I *feel* this rough, I have no interest in seeing what I *look* like.

I pass the shower and the deep jet tub and step inside the tiled cubicle with the toilet.

The good news is that I don't think we left the suite. That means we couldn't have done anything too embarrassing. Right?

Images float through my mind of the strip poker afterparty

and getting up close and personal with Shift and Flash. Damn, those boys are all kinds of fine.

Lark too.

Although I can't remember if she joined us...

Yeah, she did. She watched from the sidelines for the first round, and then Flash brought her to bed.

He mostly kept her to himself, while Shift and I focused on one another. I square off to relieve my bladder, but thinking about sex with those three is doing me no favors in getting the job done.

I force the memory of sexplay and orgasms out of my mind and focus on the veining of the tile behind the toilet. Better.

With my body clinging to the post-poker hangover, I deal with the call of nature before heading back into the main area to wash up and see what I can salvage of my dignity.

That's when I realize I'm not alone. I freeze in my tracks, my sleep-addled brain taking a moment to register the sight before me.

The door to the shower is open and Lark is standing there in all her ebony winged glory. When she hears me and turns, the breath is literally sucked from my lungs. "Damn, yer beautiful."

She's breathtaking, her body glistening with sweat. "Sorry. I had morning training with Dune and Tundra. I thought everyone was still asleep."

I take a few steps closer, drawn to her and unable to fight the pull. "Not a problem. I, uh... I'm just getting up."

Her eyes drop to my crotch and a teasing smile curls on her lips. "Yes, you are."

My cat lets off a low growl, and I pad closer. "Ye can't look at me like that if ye don't want me to devour ye, lass. I may look like a man, but I'm equal parts predator."

Even in the dim light, my feline night vision catches the flare of her pupils dilating. "If you're the predator, does that make me your prey?"

Hells yes, it does.

Damn. The animal attraction between us has been growing for weeks. We've both been busy with our bonded mates, her with the three and me mostly with Shift, but the lines are blurring. There's been a bit of sharing, but I've yet to have the pleasure of having her all to myself.

"Don't tease me, little bird. Ye see how badly I want this. If yer not there yet or ye want to focus on the others, ye need to tell me now."

"And if I want you? If I've lain awake, thinking about you... if I feel the animalistic wildness of your cat and I want to be your prey... what then?"

I take another two prowling steps, closing the distance between us. "Then all ye have to do is give me the word. Ask me to fuck ye in the shower. Tell me to spread ye open on the counter and lick yer cream until ye come undone. Yer the one who holds the cards here, little bird."

Her nipples peak and she gives off a wafting scent of arousal that nearly breaks my control. "Fuck me in the shower, Mac. Let your cat out to play with its little bird. Devour me."

"Done."

In two striding steps, I have her off the ground, and her feet wrapped around my hips. Her wings flare behind her shoulders and my cat pounces forward. Need radiates through me like fire as she holds me close. My skin prickles as her hands explore every inch of my arms, shoulders, and then sink into my hair.

Pressing her against the wall of the shower, I free one hand and start the spray of water. She squeals as the cold spray hits, but then melts against me as the temperature warms.

She's beautiful, radiant even, her skin glowing after a warrior's workout. When her head drops back, she lets off a breathy sigh. "Yes. Finally."

I nip at the flesh of her neck, tasting the salty sweat of her workout and love it. "Finally?"

Her fingers tighten in my hair, and the pull is sharp. She's not kidding around here. "Yes. I've wanted to have you all to myself for ages. I love the boys, but they treat me like a queen. I have a wild side. I feel the pull of your cat and I need him to take what he needs."

My mind fritzes out and my cat rises to the surface so fast I almost lose control of my form. But no. Lark wants to be fucked by the man as well as ravaged by the beast within.

The hot water envelops us, steam filling the room, but it's her that has me on fire. We stand there, crushed together under the cascading water, our hands grabbing, our mouths seeking.

I was prepared to take my time and give her butterfly kisses and all the romantic prep ladies love, but that's not what she's asking for.

She wants raw passion.

The cascading water beating down on us turns the room into a cocoon of steam and heat. With my grip on her thighs, I shift until the crown of my cock is lined up in her heat. "Fuck, yer slick and I haven't even spent the time to get you ready fer me."

"I told you. I *am* ready. I'm more than ready." Gripping my shoulders, she digs her nails into my flesh and flashes me a challenging look. "Come on, wildcat. Devour your little bird."

This woman is going to be the death of me.

My cat lets off a savage snarl and then I'm pushing into her, pressing her against the unyielding marble of the shower wall.

"Yes!" she groans, her voice strained.

We've only just started, but the muscles of her pussy are throbbing around me, grabbing my length with a greedy pull.

It's fucking heaven.

Our eyes never leave each other as I slam into her. I'm not being a gentleman because that's not what she wants from me. She wants feral.

If she wants the beast, I'll give it to her.

Honestly, it's incredible to let him out to play. Where my cat's influence on my sex life leads to a lot of tease and play, if he's truly allowed to let loose, he is wild.

Women sometimes say they want me to let him free, but most don't mean it or don't understand what that means.

Lark is different.

I'm letting loose on her, and the scent of her arousal keeps keying up hotter and hotter. The feminine scent is mixing with the warm torrent steaming the air and I'm practically drunk on it.

I can't get enough.

Stepping back from the wall, I pause for a moment and let her feet drop to the shower floor. Her whimper of disapproval is too fucking cute.

"Trust me, little bird. I'm just switching positions so I can get in deeper." Spinning her to face the wall, I press a hand against her back and bend her over. "Yer still loving rough and dirty?"

"Yes," she gasps.

"Then brace yourself, lass, because I'm going to fuck ye so hard, ye'll feel me inside ye for a week."

She gets her hands up and her arms braced in a split second, and I stifle a chuckle. "Good girl. Such a hungry, horny girl. You ready for this?"

"Yes."

I believe her.

I take a moment to prime her with my fingers, knowing that withdrawal and reentry can get tender. Shit. She's so fucking wet.

My fingers slide through her drenched folds, and I make sure she's good and wound up before I slide into her for round two.

Standing behind her, with my hands gripping her hips, I'm struck by the sheen of her ebony wings.

So. Fucking. Beautiful.

My hips rock into her without conscious thought. It's like I was made to fuck this woman. She checks all my boxes and drives me absolutely wild.

The slap of flesh builds as I get back to business and thrust in deeper than I could before. Each time my hips meet her ass, she lets off a throaty grunt.

She's holding off.

I feel how greedy her pussy is, and she's so close. My cock is being milked with every stroke of in and out. It's delicious agony because there's no way I'm going off first and she's fighting her release with everything she's got.

"Let yerself fall, Lark. I promise I'm not finished. I'll fuck ye all morning. I'll fill ye with my cum and then bathe ye clean and fill ye again and again."

Her head drops forward and a glorious cry peals from her throat. "Yes. Don't stop! Don't ever stop!"

As her orgasm takes hold, I'm lost to the sensation.

So tight. So hot.

I follow her into the freefall of bliss, slamming forward as my cat roars and my seed spills into her. The deep scent of spice bleeding from my skin is no surprise. My cat claimed her weeks ago.

And now, I have, too.

This female is my female.

We may have been bound to the three and brought together against our will, but the fae universe knew what it was doing because Lark is mine.

As the last of my tremors ease, I wrap my arm around her waist and help her straighten. My spent cock slides out of her, and I miss her snug warmth immediately.

Turning her in my arms, I meet her lips and try to convey in a kiss how incredible I think she is. "Ye shattered me, little bird. Ye wound me up like no other and ye left me humbled. Yer incredible."

Her eyes are filled with desire, her lips parting as she captures my mouth in a fervent kiss. Even after the wildness of what we just shared, the taste of her, the feel of her, it consumes me. "You're pretty incredible yourself, Mac. Whatever powers brought us together, they got it so right."

I chuckle. "I was just thinkin' the same thing."

Breaking away from the kiss, I trail my lips down her neck to her collarbone. Her head tips back, a soft moan escaping her lips, the sound reverberating through me, fueling my desire for her.

As our bodies sink together, everything else fades away. The heat, the steam, the cascading water, all amplify the sensations, wrapping us in a world of our own.

Her nails rake down my back as the tension between us builds, her breaths becoming shallower, her body moving more urgently against mine.

I hold her close as my need for her returns and my body hardens against her soft curves. "I believe I promised to fuck ye all morning."

A deep chuckle rumbles at the base of her throat. "I believe you did."

I press a gentle kiss to her forehead, wrapping my arms around her in a tender embrace. "Well then, let me prove to ye that I'm a man of my word."

Her smile is as sexy and relaxed as I've ever seen. "That sounds perfect."

It does. And for this moment, there is no battle to fight, no enemy to defeat. There is just us, finding solace in each other's arms, hidden away in our own steam-filled heaven.

CHAPTER EIGHT

Lark

The grand staircase of Amberloq Hall winds in an open spiral, creating a column of space from the ceiling of the top floor all the way to the grand entrance below. This building was designed to house Elbirfae warriors, and this is the fastest and easiest way to the ground floor.

Hopping over the balustrade, I drop and open my wings to slow my descent. The pull of gravity and the wind blowing my hair and my feathers boosts my renewed energy.

Even as I leave the boys lounging in our suite, Mac's touch still lingers on my skin, a sexy reminder of our shared intimacy. And that's to say nothing of the fun we all had last night.

My boots barely make a sound as I land, and then I'm making my way through Amberloq Hall, heading toward the back lawn. From the window of our suite, I saw Dune and Tundra working drills with the trainees out on the training grounds.

The heat of the midday air is a sweltering contrast to when I was working out early this morning, but I'm greeted by more than the temperature. "Hello, Moonshade. How are you, sweet girl?"

The ebony and silver wolf bonded to Shadow races over to welcome me to the gallery of onlookers. I scrub my fingers through the thick fur of her scruff and stroke her ears. After sufficient love, she trots back to where Shadow and Honor are sitting in the gazebo, watching the trainees practice.

I follow her wagging tail toward the empty seats. "Do you mind if I join you?"

Shadow rises to his feet and gestures toward the nearest chair. "Of course not. Please, sit."

I haven't had more than a few polite encounters in the hall with Honor's fourth mate, because unlike Lukas, Dune, and Tundra, Shadow isn't a warrior.

Or at least, not in the soldier sense of the word.

From what I've heard and seen, though, he is a warrior against the setbacks of life.

"Please, sit," I say, settling into the chair nearest to Honor. "How are they doing?"

Honor's gaze scans across the lawn and she smiles at the sight of our teenaged and applicant warriors training by the pond. "They've been through an ordeal, their resolve tested, and yet here they are - resilient and unwavering."

Oh good. That's what I see too, but I'm biased and want them all to succeed. We need strength on the Amberloq force, and they need somewhere to focus on harnessing their anger and loss of control over the past two years. "They're a great bunch of kids."

Shadow nods. "I agree. I've spoken with each of them and they're doing very well. You should be quite proud."

"Me? I didn't do much."

Shadow's blind gaze passes over me. He may not have conventional sight, but I'd swear he sees right through me. "You were their protector when they needed one, their mentor through their ordeal, and their example to follow once reintegrated into quadrant life."

"Yeah, you were," Honor says, grinning. "Their successes are your successes. Take the compliment."

I'm not going to argue.

"So, did you just come out here to check on our young warriors?" Honor asks.

I scan the group, doing formations by the pond, and shake my head. "No. I saw you sitting out here and wanted to check in."

"I shall give you some privacy," Shadow says, rising to his feet again.

"Oh, no. I don't want to chase you off," I say.

"Nonsense. Moonshade is getting antsy, and I promised her a walk in the forest. The two of you enjoy yourselves and we'll be back in a while." He leans in and gives Honor a kiss before he and his wolf are jogging across the back lawn toward the trees.

"Is it rude of me to say how amazed I always am when I see him navigating the world around him?"

Honor chuckles. "No. That's not rude at all. Shadow's loss of sight was a shock, and it could have gone really badly, but since the moment Lukas brought him Moonshade, the two have bonded and Shadow's world of sight was returned to him."

"So, he truly sees out Moonshade's eyes?"

"Yes."

"That's incredible."

"Usually. Although he gets annoyed when he's kissing me and she's licking her butt or eating a toad."

I burst out laughing. "I see how that could dampen his enjoyment."

The two of us chuckle about that for a moment, and then Honor looks at me and smiles. "He's right, though, you know."

"Who, Shadow?"

She nods. "The kids have become strong, just like their

leader. They follow your example and you've done an exceptional job handling everything that's been thrown at you."

I blow out a long breath. "Thank you for saying so, but 'thrown at me' is pretty accurate. From the moment your mates raided the goblin camp, it feels like my life has been spinning out of my control."

"I know that feeling. That's me most of the time."

"That's not how it looks from the outside."

"Excellent. It shouldn't." She captures a long strand of silver hair blowing against her face and tucks it behind her ear. "One of the first things my father taught Creed and me was that as leaders of the people, we needed to always appear in full control, even if we weren't."

I get that. "No one wants to know the people in charge are losing their minds."

"Exactly. And you do it very well, by the way. We've all admired the way you've taken the reins of leadership, your commitment to the realm, and especially your mating bonds. From the outside, it looks like you've got it all under control."

I sit back in my chair and think about that. "Things seem to be falling into place."

"Personally, or professionally?"

"Both, I think. Dune and Tundra have been wonderful about my Amberloq training, Lukas has been great about tactical strategy, and the guys are really gelling."

Honor nods. "How's Link?"

"Better, I think. According to the scientists, Doc, and Shift, he's simply in healing stasis and can wake any time. In fact, last night when I was sitting with him, I would've sworn I could feel him trying to get back to us."

She stares out at Dune and Tundra working with the trainees and smiles. "What about the personal stuff: the bonding, having four mates thrust at you all at once? How are you adapting to that?"

I sit back and study her. "Are you asking as my boss? Is there something I should know? Do you think I'm blurring some line with the three and losing objectivity?"

She chuckles. "I'm sure there are blurred lines, but no, our super soldiers have proven themselves. I'm asking as your friend. How are things?"

Images of the past twenty-four hours pass through my mind, and I try not to blush. "Having four mates isn't something I ever expected."

Honor laughs. "Trust me. I was raised with the possibility, and it still threw me. Four guys are a lot to juggle. A lot of personalities. A lot of testosterone."

"A lot of sex," I say before my brain can catch up with my mouth.

Honor snorts and doubles forward, laughing. "So much cock."

"Right?" The two of us sit there giggling for a bit, letting that sink in. "Not that I'm complaining."

"Hell no. No complaints. It's just a lot. I get it."

I know she does. "Link is still our biggest hurdle. I need him to wake up so we can start integrating him into what we're building."

"But Flash and Shift are committed to this either way, right?"

I nod. "Yeah. Flash, Shift, Mac, and I are having a lot of fun, but there's also a deep connection there. It seems we've all been adrift for too long, and now our souls are anchored to one another. Does that make sense?"

Honor sighs. "Perfectly."

As the young warriors continue their training, Dune and Tundra break away from the drills and jog over to join us.

"Hey, Lark," Dune says, leaning in to kiss Honor. "Hey, babe. Are you enjoying the view?"

"How could I not?"

Dune straightens and Tundra takes her hand and kisses her

knuckles. "So, what do you think of the potential of the trainees?

"I'm impressed," she says, her gaze assessing the warriors moving through rotations out on the lawn. "They're strong, they follow instruction well, and they're focused. I think they all look like warriors we can work with."

"We'll still need to complete the trials," Tundra says. "Once we find Brass and bring our lost home, we'll have time to focus on building the Amberloq."

Honor squeezes his hand in hers and stands. "We'll find them. And when we bring them home, we'll throw an enormous party, and we'll bring in all of Yarko's favorite foods from the Human Realm."

I know Tundra is heartbroken over the disappearance of his charge and I want to believe Honor when she says we'll get them back, but I'm not as hopeful as she is.

The Gen-3 tore Alpha's head off.

They came to destroy us. I don't think Beta is in a holding cell somewhere waiting for us to save him. I think he was likely dead days ago when he first went missing. We just haven't found him.

And as for Skye and Yarko... What use would they serve to Brass and his team? I hope I'm wrong and I'm just being cynical, but I don't think I am.

It won't do anyone any good for me to voice that opinion, so I change the topic. "Have we gotten anywhere on interrogating the Gen-3 soldiers we captured? Do we have any idea where Brass is?"

Honor sighs. "Lukas and Rhylan have been trying to interrogate them for days. The Gen-3 seem to have a system shut down that activates when captured. They went offline as soon as their capture was imminent, and we haven't been able to wake them up."

I stretch my neck and try to loosen the tension building in

my shoulders. "Do we need them awake? They've got system ports, don't they? Can't we just plug in and, I don't know... download what we want from them?"

Dune gestures to me and nods. "See. I'm not the only one who thinks so."

Honor shakes her head. "From what we know, the Gen-3 soldiers aren't much different from Flash, Shift, and Link. The difference is that their directives were been tampered with, so instead of loyalty to the Crown of Dornte, their loyalty is to Brass and his backers."

"What does that have to do with a forced download?" I scan their faces, not understanding.

"Josie and the castle scientists believe Brass programmed safeguards against forced download. They believe it'll end them."

"Seriously? After what they did to Alpha and Link and what they might do to our missing friends, do we care if there are a few less Gen-3? Isn't it worth trying if it could end all this?"

Honor comes over to me and squeezes my shoulders. "Lark, think about it. We're in virgin territory here. On behalf of the crown, my aunt instigated a program to create bio-engineered super soldiers. The Gen-3s aren't the only result of that program. We also have Flash, Link, Shift, and Beta."

My mind is trying to put the pieces together, but I'm still not getting it.

"Creed and I have been working on how to give your mates autonomy within the realm. We have to declare our stance on the soldiers Brass created. Either they are sentient beings, or they are robotic property."

I stiffen. "They're sentient. My guys live and laugh and love and they want to build a life serving the quadrant. They're *not* property."

"Exactly. So, if we set the precedent that we can strap the Gen-3 down to a table and forcibly download their programming knowing it might well terminate them, that's either murder or considering them nothing more than very expensive tech."

I groan as the implications hit me. "You can't give my guys the status they deserve without extending the same considerations to *all* the soldiers created in your aunt's program."

"Right. And we don't know... maybe we can access the proper way to realign the programming of the Gen-3 and return them to the aim of serving Dornte. We can't write them off or destroy them yet."

As much as I hate the idea of the Gen-3s getting this much consideration when they don't deserve it, I see her point. "It just sucks that doing the right thing is actually making our job harder."

Honor nods. "I agree. One hundred percent. So, why don't you grab your guys and head to the castle? Maybe between all of you, we can figure out a way to find Brass without lobotomizing the Gen-3s."

CHAPTER NINE

Flash

The security door to the Thornebane Castle war room swings open, and I step back to let the others pass. Mac and Lark head inside and I follow. In the center of the room, Rhylan and Lukas are standing at the large table, their faces cast in sharp relief by the light of the holographic images floating above it.

"Good. You're here." Rhylan greets without looking over, his focus riveted on the maps and faces floating before him.

He swipes his hand in a practiced motion, manipulating the images. He sends the images of two men to the side and enlarges the map.

"Been busy, have ye, lads?" Mac asks, moving into position next to Lukas.

I admire the ease with which he fits into any situation. Where I often feel awkward and watch to take social cues, Mac's nature makes it look effortless.

Lukas grunts, shooting his friend a sidelong glance. "Brass isn't going to find himself."

"That would be nice though," I say.

Mac winks at me and grins. "Aye, it would. Still, it's likely best we don't hold our breath."

Lark moves to stand opposite Rhylan and studies the information on and above the table. There's a certain steeliness in her gaze this afternoon.

When she came out of the steamy bathroom this morning, she had a glow about her that made her seem soft and content. Then she went out to oversee the trainees and came back with a determined set to her jaw. "Have we got any leads?"

"A few." Rhylan points to the faces along the right side. "We've homed in on several of the one percenters who we suspect are funding Brass."

"Do we know where they live?"

Rhylan nods. "We do, but they're not the kind of people you can drop in on unannounced. If we raid their homes, we've gotta be damned sure we can tie them to Brass."

"How do we do that?" I ask.

"We brainstorm," Mac says. "Rhy has been following the money trail to Brass' backers, but if we barge into their homes and they have excuses for how the money got to Brass, it's Creed who will pay."

Rhylan nods. "And seeing how we suspect most of these same people of also funding the raids by the Usurper Queen and the Blood Witch, we'd rather not have a repeat performance."

"So, we focus on tracking Brass down," Lark says. "If we find Brass, we bring him down, and put an end to his twisted games."

For a moment, there's no sound as the group considers that, and then we all nod our agreement.

"All right, brainstorming ways to find Brass," Lukas says. "We've already fed the likenesses of the Gen-3 soldiers, the scientists, and Brass himself into the municipal cameras around the city."

Rhylan touches the map and hundreds of blue dots light up.

"We also had Keyla go into the tunnels below the city and leave word with the folks who live in the underground to let us know if they see or hear anything."

I frown. "It sounds like it's a passive search. The only way we can advance our position is in response to someone getting caught by a camera or noticed by one of our informants."

"For right now, yes," Rhylan says.

"I'd rather take an offensive position," I say.

The dragon nods. "As would we all. The question is, what's our thread to pull that will unravel the tapestry of Brass' world?"

"The serum," I say, my voice ringing in the hushed room. All eyes shift to me. "Unlike us, Brass created the Gen-3 soldiers out of living beings. He uses the serum to contain their emotions and to prevent their pre-program personalities from surfacing."

Mac grins. "Keep goin', lad. We're with ye."

"Well, we know Brass needs the serum because he returned to the bunker and tried to fight us for it."

"And if he's burned through it, he can't stabilize his Gen-3 army," Lark adds.

Lukas meets Rhylan's gaze, and then the dragon taps his fingers over the surface of the table. "And without the serum, they'll become unstable. I'm establishing a program that will alert us to any violent events within the city limits."

"Did Josie and the scientists get a chemical breakdown of the serum?" Lukas asks.

Rhylan finishes what he's doing and then pulls up a list of components and chemical ingredients.

"Are any of these rare?" Lark asks. "If he has to replicate the serum, he'll need to source out the components to make more."

"And if they're rare, we'll be able to track them more easily than if they are not," I say.

A murmur of assent ripples around the room.

It's a starting point.

Rhylan claps his hands together, a new energy radiating from him. "All right, people. Let's divvy up these components and find out where they can be sourced, and who's been buying them."

As the war room bursts into a flurry of activity, I can't help but feel a rush of adrenaline. We've got a plan and a sense of purpose.

Flash, are you at the castle?

I zone out the buzz of voices around me and focus on Shift. *I am. Is everything all right?*

I need you to bring Doc back to our suite.

What happened?

Link is awake.

~

Link

A hazy fog dissipates from my consciousness and the oppressive weight of my healing stasis lifts. My ocular receptors come online, and I sit up with a sharp gasp. My systems are back online, every sensor buzzing with activity, returning signals of function and stability.

Where am I?

"Shift! Flash! Where are you, my brothers?"

"I'm here."

The sound of Shift's reply in the next room calms me more than I ever thought possible. Flipping the sheet off my legs, I swing my feet to the floor to seek him out.

"What are you doing? Brother, you need to stay in bed." Shift rushes in and presses a hand on my shoulder, forcing me back toward the mattress. "You suffered a great deal of physical and system damage in the explosion. Lay still until you can be examined properly."

"Explosion?"

"Yes, at the Mount Hekko lodge. Several of our trial applicants were Gen-3 infiltrators Brass sent to destroy us. What do you remember?"

My systems are still spinning, making it difficult to focus. "I was with Beta. We were in pursuit of..." I meet my brother's gaze as the last moments before the explosion play out in my mind. "The Gen-3 had Alpha. They took him and were trying to remove his data chip. Alpha fought and they..."

Shift locks his gaze with mine. "We could not repair him. Alpha has been terminated."

Terminated? Maybe it's because I just woke up, but I can't reconcile that in my mind.

Even after seeing it happen...

A surge of anxiety overwhelms me, and my stabilization sensors fail. I reach out a hand to support myself on the bed. "Where are Flash and Beta? Are they well?"

Shift draws a deep breath. "Flash is at the castle, working with the others to locate Brass. Beta is missing. When the smoke of the explosions cleared, Beta, Skye, and Yarko were unaccounted for."

I raise my hand and rub at the pressure in my chest. The white feathered Elbirfae girl? I like her. She was kind to me. She taught me, Alpha, and Beta how to play pool. She was my partner.

"What is being done to find them?" I ask, making another attempt to get out of bed.

Once again, Shift rebukes my attempt. "Not yet, brother. Doc is on his way. Let us examine you. There were things we didn't understand about the way your system responded to the damage you withstood."

I understand his concern. Even now, I do not feel myself.

Still, lying in this bed is making me feel alarmingly vulnerable and I don't like it.

Not at all.

"Shift, you're a healer," I rasp out, my voice echoing oddly in my own ears. "Look at me. You can see I am well."

He presses a firm hand to my chest. "You will lay back or we will have a problem."

I roll my eyes. His overprotectiveness can be such an annoyance at times. I'm about to tell him as much when the door bursts open.

The commotion floods my senses as Lark, Mac, and Flash come barreling into the room, trailing a burly, dark-haired man in their wake. The sight is enough to momentarily stall my protests, my chest tightening at the sight of their relieved faces.

"Well, look who finally rejoined the land of the livin'." Mac grins, crossing his arms over his chest as he leans against the end of the bed.

"Link, you had us worried." Lark rushes to close the distance between us. Without hesitation, she leans over, falling against my chest to hug me.

I am unprepared for the sudden familiarity, although I enjoy her warmth and the feel of her curves pressed against me. Her heart races as she takes comfort from our embrace.

When she eases back and sits on the side of the mattress, her face is flushed, and her eyes are wide and shining with emotion.

It's an attractive look on her.

It makes my circuits hum in response.

"How are you? Can we get you anything?"

I'm not sure what she sees in my reaction, but her excitement dims. "What's wrong?" she asks.

"Nothing. Well, other than my brother refusing to allow me to get out of this bed."

She shakes her head. "No. It wasn't that."

I'm not sure what has upset her, but I'm less sure why I care... but I *do* care. "Have I done something?"

"You look surprised to see us," she says. "Or surprised we were panicked about you?"

"Perhaps he is simply disoriented," Flash offers. "He woke up in strange surroundings and didn't realize we had moved into our suite in the Amberloq Hall. Is that it, brother? You didn't realize we now live on the grounds of Thornebane Castle?"

Thornebane Castle? I blink, hoping my processors catch up with my mental spiral. "You are correct, Flash. I didn't realize that."

I let them take from that what they will because Lark is not wrong. When they rushed in here, I was surprised—not by their presence, but by the intensity of their relief.

They seem genuinely pleased to find me awake.

I expected that from Shift and Flash, but Mac and Lark? I thought neither of them liked me much.

And I don't even know the man standing behind them. Still, he looks glad to see me.

When I meet the gaze of the man standing by the door, he steps forward. "Hello, Link. My name is Doctor Dillan Baskins, but most people around here just call me Doc."

"The bear shifter from the Human Realm, mated as part of the royal four," I say, placing him.

He nods. "That's me. But before all that, I was a military doctor and surgeon. When you were first brought back to the castle grounds, I was one of the physicians called in to assess your condition."

I dip my chin. "When I was first brought in? How long ago was that?"

"You arrived five days ago."

Five days. I draw a deep breath and try to access my internal systems. "Why don't I have access to the passing of time? What's wrong with my systems? Why can't I connect with Flash and Shift?"

My questions come out in a bombardment, and I regret how panicked I sound. I glance away, my gaze panning the sparse, impersonal room around us. "I can't feel them. It's like they're... they're just gone."

I can't look at my brothers, or Mac, or Lark. I don't want to see whatever concern or pity might be in their eyes.

Doc moves into my line of sight, and I see nothing but intelligence and understanding. "We're looking into all that. Now that you're awake, we'll give you a thorough once over and compare the results to what we've recorded over the past few days and to what's in your specifications database. I won't speculate. We'll gather the facts and assess once we know more."

That makes sense.

I never thought I'd say this about a human stranger, but I like this man.

"Very well. What do you need me to do?"

CHAPTER TEN

Shift

The hum of energy in the Amberloq war room is like a living thing as Mac, Flash, and I join Lukas and Rhylan. They stand at the table in the center of the room, poring over holographic maps and intel on our upcoming mission.

"Is Lark joining us?" Lukas asks.

"No. She thought I would be of greater value on this mission and sent me in her place," I say.

Flash shakes his head. "She wanted to spend time alone with Link and care for him."

"How is Link?" Lukas asks, lifting his gaze from the data he's studying.

"Better," Mac says. "He's awake and both Shift and Doc think he's over the worst of it."

His gaze narrows. "But?"

"But he is still experiencing system issues," I answer. "His stabilization system isn't calibrating properly and his communication channels don't seem to function at all."

"And in normal speak, that means?"

"He's unsteady on his feet and he can't speak to Flash, Lark, and I through our mental channel."

"And the odds of that clearing up on a system recalibration or diagnostic?"

I shake my head. "There is a disconnect which I have yet to figure out."

"Would working with Josie and the schematics we confiscated from the bunker help?"

"It would, but it would be far more beneficial if I had access to the tools his scientists used."

Lukas frowns. "You were given everything we collected when you first arrived and needed to stabilize him."

"Brass has what we need," Flash says, leaning into his palms on the table. "He escaped the bunker with almost two dozen genetically enhanced soldiers. There's no way he fled without the specialized equipment he needs to maintain their optimal function."

Mac scrubs a hand over the russet stubble shadowing his jaw. "So, we find Brass and we help put Humpty Dumpty back together again."

"I don't understand the reference," I say.

Mac waves away my confusion. "Och, sorry. It's a reference to a Human Realm story. I meant that finding Brass helps us help Link."

"As if we needed more incentive," Tundra says, storming in with Dune. "I hear we have a starting point. What's our plan?"

Lukas points to a chemical diagram floating over the table. "The quadrant scientists isolated a unique component of the Gen-3 serum. Since it isn't readily available, finding out who's been buying it from where is our best chance to tracking down Brass and the Gen-3 army he still has at his disposal."

"Where is it being sold?" Dune asks.

"Three locations. Two in the city center—a lab and an elixir shop—and one near the Fringe." Lukas finishes with the chemical component and calls up the map. "We'll start local and then, if we strike out, those of you with wings can fly out to the Fringe."

"So, what are we looking for, exactly?" Mac asks.

Rhylan opens a drawer and holds up a small vial containing a luminescent pink liquid. "Pretty, isn't it?"

Mac snorts. "And that's what keeps the feral super soldiers from Hulking out? It looks like a shot of cotton candy."

Lukas chuckles. "You're not drinking it. You're keeping Gen-3s from acquiring it."

Rhylan points to a location on one of the maps. "If you get a chance while you're checking out your target locations, swing by here. There have been several reports of an increase in violent activity since last night. I'm thinking maybe one of Brass' soldiers is going off the rails."

Lukas and Mac exchange a look and the two of them nod. "All right, boys," Lukas says. "Grab your weapon of choice and get ready to roll out."

Rhylan points a remote toward the far wall and the front panels slide out of the way, revealing rows and rows of tactical assault weapons. "I realize you two are walking weapons, but it never hurts to add a little firepower to the assault."

Mac is the first to the weapons locker and I smile inwardly, seeing his glee as he caresses the selection like a flirting lover. "Och, aren't ye just the most beautiful lass," he says, choosing a large-barreled gun.

Dune and Tundra arrived fully armed, so they move to stand near the door.

Flash chooses a semi-automatic phaser with a chest strap, and I follow his lead. After the two of us slide a couple of extra charge cartridges into the thigh pocket of my tactical pants, Rhylan hands each of us earpieces to access his comm system.

And then, we're ready to move out.

"Have fun, kids. Stay out of trouble," Rhylan says.

The six of us stride up the long hallway in the castle's basement, climb the stairs to the main floor, and then Lukas leads us out an exit to a parking lot lined with black tactical vehicles.

Lukas tosses a set of keys to Mac and then presses the fob of another. "Dune and Tundra with me. Shift and Flash, you're with Mac."

The six of us split up and veer toward our respective vehicles.

Flash slides into the back seat and I climb in opposite Mac. I watch as he pulls the strap of nylon across his chest and latches the tether at his hip.

Flash and I do the same.

"I assume we press this button to release the harness?" Flash says, frowning down at his side.

"Och, right. Sorry, boys. This is yer first drive, isn't it? I forget sometimes how little ye've experienced. Aye, Flash, push the button and it'll release yer belt. Both of ye give it a go, if it makes ye feel better."

I do, and it actually makes me feel better.

"Must I wear this?"

Mac casts a sideways glance and meets my question with a smile. "Not if ye don't want to, soldier boy. Yer a great deal more durable than I am. If we get into a chase or one of yer evil cousins throws the truck into the side of a building, ye'll sit up and walk out of the rubble. I won't."

I don't like the sound of that at all. "Then I wish for you to wear your safety tether."

Mac winks. "I'm with ye on that. Don't worry."

When Lukas pulls out of his parking spot, Mac follows without hesitation. "Lukas has been your brother-in-arms for a long time."

Mac nods. "Aye. I guess it's been… almost fifteen years now. Why? What makes ye say that?"

"You might not have genetic enhancements tying you to one another, but you have written your own programming to work as one. You speak to one another with only a look. You know what the other is about to do before you do it. It is similar to what I share with my brothers, yet different."

Mac presses the indicator and turns to follow the taillights of Lukas' truck. "Aye, I suppose that's true. While the three of ye have been together fer almost the same time as Lukas and me, we've shared thousands of experiences. Battles. Hostage situations. Intelligence missions. Social engagements. Relationships. Loss of family. Those kinds of moments create a bond. I suppose it's very much like programming."

Yes, I suppose it is.

"I'm happy you had someone to share those moments with," Flash says from the back seat. "Having my brothers has given me a strength I don't know I would've had otherwise."

I smile and look out the window, taking in the city. "I feel the same way."

As we approach the Dornte city center, its grandeur unfolds before us. This isn't a typical fae city with meadows and woodlands. No, Dornte is a modern and marvelous testament to adaptability and innovation.

Skyscrapers shimmer like gigantic quartz crystals under the glow of the twin moons. The ethereal light casts a surreal ambiance over the cityscape, lending an almost dreamlike quality to it. Each building combines the organic elegance of fae design with the cutting-edge tech of a modern metropolis.

Bustling streets are filled with a mix of fae races, their laughter and conversation filling the night air with a lively hum.

Night markets spill onto the sidewalks, offering a rainbow of sights, scents, and sounds. Faeries flutter between stalls, their wings aglow with bioluminescence, adding a sprinkle of magic to the urban landscape.

"It's breathtaking," I say, moved to see such a different side of life. "Everyone seems so happy."

Lukas pulls the vehicle ahead of us into a parking lot and Mac follows. "Aye, much happier now than when I first arrived. The citizens weren't safe or free under the reign of Laryssa. With Creed, though, they have a good life."

Mac turns off the vehicle and the three of us get out and join the others.

"Everybody locked and loaded?" Lukas asks.

We are.

As we strike off, Dune leads the way, and we navigate the streets to the first location. Apparently, Dornte is not just a city of beauty and light, it is also a city of hidden alleyways and shadowy corners.

We weave through the city, our senses on high alert, our focus locked on tracking down the seller of the rare serum component, to find Brass and put a stop to his madness.

It's funny. Since Lark and Mac first discovered us in the bunker only weeks ago, whenever there are people around, they always stare at us.

We are the freaks.

The machines.

The abominations.

Except out here, people barely take notice of us and those who do are more interested in Dune and Tundra as the Elbirfae Biome Generals or Mac and Lukas as humans in the Fae Realm.

Flash and I don't seem to draw attention.

Brass designed us to blend in with the citizenry as part of our purpose to serve as spies within the realm. We are much more visually similar to the members of this realm than Alpha and Beta... but I suppose less so than the Gen-3 soldiers, as they were created directly from living citizens.

Before turning a corner, Dune twists to speak over his

shoulders. "Keep your wits about you, boys. We're approaching the viper's nest."

Flash stiffens, concern etched on his face. Vipers? What do snakes have to do with the serum?

"Metaphorical vipers, Flash," Mac clarifies, amusement dancing in his eyes. "He's just reminding us to stay alert."

We arrive at an unassuming shop tucked away between two larger buildings. A flickering sign above the door reads 'Exotic Elixirs' in haphazard lettering.

"All right," Lukas says. "Dune, you're with me. The rest of you are on building exterior. Mac, you've got the entrance. Tundra, check for a back exit. Shift and Flash, blend in with the crowd nearby and use your skills to gather intel."

With our duties assigned, we split up and take our positions among the people of Dornte.

Flash and I move into a sea of partygoers, revelers of the night in the throbbing heart of the city. Their energy is infectious, the vibrancy of life humming around us like an electric current.

The aroma of street food vendors wafts through the air, a melange of tempting scents that curl around us, tantalizing and unfamiliar. We hadn't had the luxury of such indulgence before Lark and Mac freed us from that bunker.

Before that, sustenance was always more about function than taste.

And then there are the people.

The people of Dornte are perhaps the most fascinating aspect of this vibrant city. So diverse, so different from us. The range of their emotions is almost overwhelming, a swirling cacophony of feelings we are only just beginning to understand.

Laughter bubbles up from the crowd, rich and infectious, a testament to the joys of social connection. Soft whispers of shared secrets, heated words of passionate debate, hushed tones of intimate conversations—the city is a breathing entity, pulsating with the vibrancy of its inhabitants.

My brothers and I have spent so long isolated from the world that the sheer variety of interaction is a novel experience.

Flash's eyes flicker from face to face, taking it all in, the same curiosity mirrored in my gaze.

We are here to blend in, to observe, to understand, and maybe, in some small way, to learn what it means to be part of this bustling, chaotic, captivating world.

We are strangers to this, but tonight, under the glow of the twin moons, we are simply two more souls caught up in the rhythm of Dornte.

CHAPTER ELEVEN

Lark

"Link. Talk to me." I'm sitting on the end of the bed in his room, waiting for him to come out of the washroom. I've gotten nothing but the silent treatment since the moment he lost his balance and I dared to stop him from face planting on the carpet.

The water turns off, but still nothing.

"Link, seriously. You just woke after a catastrophic event. It's perfectly normal that you're not functioning at a hundred percent."

He steps out of the bathroom, his hips bound by a towel, his glare dark with fury. "No, it's not perfectly normal! I was created with a system recalibration and regenerative programming. It's not natural at *all* for me to wake five days after being injured and still be exhibiting glitches."

I sigh. "You got up. You got dizzy. As glitches go, it could've been worse. Let's try to keep things in perspective."

He grabs at the stack of clothing I set out for him and drops the towel. "All right, Lark. Let's put things into perspective. I'm a soldier. How do I battle if my stabilization is off? How do I move through a crowd unseen if I'm tripping and bumping into people? How do I perform my fucking directives if my 'could be worse' glitches continue?"

Yeah, fair point.

"Like Doc said, now that you're awake, your team of caregivers can do so much more. It just might take time."

He shoves his arms through the black t-shirt and wedges his hardened muscles into the cotton fabric. I almost feel bad for the thread straining to hold the seams together... or I would if he wasn't rocking the look like a total sex god.

"Why are you looking at me like that?"

I wave my finger in the air between us. "Nuh-uh, you don't get to change the subject."

"Then this conversation is over because I am finished talking about the current subject." He shakes out the legs of his pants and stomps his feet into them, pulling them up his thighs and denying me the pleasure of seeing him naked.

I give him a moment, watching as he dresses, tracking the flex of his jaw muscles as he calms down. When I think it's safe again, I stand to face him. "All right. Let's not talk about your physical condition. Let's spend a moment on your emotional condition."

He rolls his eyes and turns to leave.

I catch his arm. Whether or not his systems are wonky, Link is much stronger than I am. That he allows me to tug him to a stop says something. "I'm sorry. I'm not trying to upset you. Believe it or not, I see that you're reeling and I'm trying to comfort you."

He won't turn to look at me, so I circle him. "Link, I think I've proven you can trust me. Let me help you."

"And what can you do? Can you recalibrate my stabilization? Can you reconnect my communication channels? No offense meant, but you don't have the skills to help me."

Ouch. Tell me how you really feel.

"Granted, I don't have the science or tech skills to help you, but I've woken up to find my world changed. I've been caught in the wake of violence and sent spinning. Maybe you're discounting my skills."

He frowns down at me. "Is this about sex?"

I let out a long breath and let my head drop forward. "No. It's not about sex. Although, I'm sure releasing some endorphins would make you feel better. What I'm offering you is companionship, understanding, and maybe some comfort in a trying time."

He stares at me like I've got two heads for a moment and then his shoulders relax, and he arches a brow. "I'm not good at this."

"I am aware."

"I've never needed comfort before. I am a superior being, crafted to be elite."

"I've read your specs. For sure, you're the man."

His brow tightens. "There is a seventy-four percent chance you didn't mean that."

I chuckle. "It's called teasing. And yes, I was teasing. I'm aware of all the things in your plus and minus columns. Even so, I'm here and I want to stand by you and help you."

He seems to consider that for a while before canting his head to one side. "And what would comforting me look like?"

"It can be as simple as a hug or we could share a meal or play a game of pool or take a walk. What do you feel up to doing?"

"I am extremely low on nutritional sustenance."

"Excellent. Then let's go down to the kitchen and get you something to eat."

His frown returns. "If we are in the Amberloq Hall, that means the other warriors are here as well, correct?"

"That's right."

"Then I wish to stay here. You could comfort me by bringing food up to this suite."

I hear the subtext and while it doesn't surprise me, it saddens me. "Link. No one will judge you for not performing at your optimum specifications. Everyone is worried about you. The kids have been asking about you. The people within these walls are your friends."

He shakes his head. "I am not so damaged that I have lost my sense of station. I neither have nor need friends. Flash and Shift stand by me because we are brothers. They are the only ones I can count on."

"Bullshit."

He frowns. "I beg your pardon?"

"You heard me. That's a pile of crap. I stayed behind from the mission tonight because there's an undercurrent of unease in you. I wanted to be here for you because that's what friends do. I care about you. How can someone so smart be so stupid as not to see that?"

Stupid? "You think I'm stupid?"

"There are different types of intelligence and right now, you're being intentionally difficult. Your systems are faulty and that's unsettling. I understand that. But I also understand you're a proud male, accustomed to being superior and always in control."

I wait to see if he wants to add anything to that, but he doesn't.

"Even before the explosion, I saw you struggle. I watched you grapple with the vulnerability of leaving the bunker and trusting new people. I recognize how hard it is for you to trust and understand why."

His shoulders stiffen, and he lifts his chin. "It's easy. I simply don't believe people deserve my trust."

His words strike me like a physical blow. "You're being an ass."

"I'm not. You asked how I feel, and I told you."

"Then you feel wrong."

He arches a brow. "How is what I feel wrong?"

I take a step back to avoid the urge to slap him. Then, I draw a deep breath and try to remind myself that he's still adapting, and he's dealing with a lot.

"Link…" I say, starting again. "I get that Brass and his people betrayed you, but I'm not them. I've been on your side from the very beginning. It's hurtful and insulting for you to say I don't deserve your trust. I'm trying here. I want to build a relationship with you."

"Why?" he snaps, his gaze narrowing.

"Why do you think?"

"I honestly don't know. You bonded with Flash and Shift, and by extension, Mac. They offer strength, companionship, physical attraction, humor, and all the components of a relationship a female might need. Why me? To round out your numbers? To appease my brothers? Four lovers seems excessive given you only have three orifices."

The slap of my hand against his cheek stings my palm only half as much as it stings my heart. "Fuck you, Link. If you think I'm pathetic enough that I'd put up with your toxic hostility because I want to have my holes filled, then hide in this room forever and rot for all I care."

The thundering boom of the door slamming behind me echoes through the corridor as I storm to the end of the hall and through the balcony doors.

With a launch, I push into the air and put as much distance as I can between Link and my urge to tackle him to the carpet and strangle him.

What a self-involved, insufferable ass.

～

Mac

I take up position on the door, digging in next to the street meat food truck at the curb. From my vantage point, I can cover the entrance to the shop selling the serum component, but also Flash and Shift milling around the crowd with matching looks of awe on their gorgeous faces.

It's damn funny, actually.

Lukas sent them into the bustling crowd to observe, but he didn't elaborate. He didn't tell them what he wanted them to be taking in, so that left them free to absorb everything.

And they're killing it.

They are quick to learn and even quicker to adapt. A furious blush floods my cheeks as memories of tangled limbs and feverish kisses resurface.

And quick to move from proficiency to prowess.

A cool breeze brushes past and I catch a scent that sends a chill up my spine. I press my fingers together and push them into my mouth and under my tongue. My shrill whistle brings both Shift's and Flash's focus back to the mission at hand.

The two of them hustle back to me damn quick. "What is it?" Shift asks.

I tap the communicator in my ear at the same time I bring Flash and Shift up to speed. "We're not alone here, boys. I caught wind of the Gen-3 soldier Link fought in the bunker raid."

"Not it," Dune says, over our comm channel.

I scoff. "Since when does our Desert Biome General back away from a fight?"

"Since I saw that fucking lion man beat the shit out of Link," Dune says.

Shift frowns. "He is a lion of the feline folk, yes, but he is still just a soldier like we are."

"Like you two are," I correct. "Dune's right. If he's as tough as

Link reported, he's an alpha beast and it'll take the two of you to take him down."

"We have to find him first," I say.

"What does he look like?" Lukas asks. "Mac, Flash, and I weren't on that floor of the bunker during the battle."

Dune answers. "He's a great leonine beast with black skin and penetrating golden eyes and a long flowing mane of ebony hair that makes him look like the heroine on the cover of a romance novel."

I laugh. "Are you crushing on him? It sounds like ye'd rather fuck him than fight him."

"Fuck you, Mac. He's pretty, all right. And no, I don't want to fight him. That was my point."

"No one is fighting anyone until we track down this serum and the Gen-3s who might be here to obtain it," Lukas says.

"Aye, we're on it. Finish inside there and join us when ye can." I tap my comm closed and turn to Flash and Shift. "Watch yer backs, lads. We still don't know what all of them look like. On yer toes."

Despite the chill, sweat beads on my brow as we spread out and scan the narrow alleys, wary of the shady characters lurking in recessed doorways and behind crates.

"Over there," Flash whispers, nodding to a group of men huddled together near a dimly lit storefront. Their furtive glances and hushed voices set off alarm bells in my head, but it's impossible to tell if they're Gen-3 or simply engaged in their own illicit dealings.

I meet Shift's gaze and tilt my head toward the alleyway. "I'm going to check out a group of unsavory locals."

As I press forward, the hair raises on the back of my neck and my cat prowls to the surface. I open the comm channel with a discreet brush of fingers through my hair and keep moving forward. "Shift and Flash. My senses tell me that unseen eyes are following me from behind. Check the shadows of the sight-lines and find the fucker."

"We're finished in here," Lukas says. "We're making our way out to you."

Adrenaline is coursing through me as I continue toward the crowd down the alley. "Double time it. I've got a bad feeling."

"Flash or Shift... anything?" Lukas asks.

"Nothing yet," Shift says.

"Flying up to the apartment rooftop across the road for a better vantage point," Flash says.

The moment a guttural growl resonates through the comms, chaos erupts.

"Report!" I turn back and race toward the street. "Who engaged?"

CHAPTER TWELVE

Link

I made her cry. My programming prepares me for battle, infiltration, seduction, intel gathering, and a hundred other scenarios. But as I stare at the back of the bedroom door, I do not know how to handle a situation where I made a woman cry.

And not in just a small way.

I insulted her character, disregarded her feelings toward me, and even after all she's done, told her she was unworthy of my trust.

"No one can say I'm subtle when I err. If I make mistakes, I make them count."

Normally when I make a social misstep, it's either intentional and I don't care who ends up angry, or if I do care, I speak to Shift or Flash for input on where I went wrong. They are so much better than me at making things right.

"I should've just gone down to the kitchen and shared a meal with her."

It's too late for that now.

Twisting the door handle, I exit the small room and end up in a private corridor with two more closed doors to choose from: one straight ahead and one to my left.

I try the door straight ahead and enter the living area of an extensive suite. The sofas are gray with navy piping. The flooring is dark wood, polished to a high shine. And beyond the seating area is a wooden table with six chairs.

Feeling like I've intruded, I'm about to retreat when I notice Flash's t-shirt slung over the back of the sofa. Scanning the large, open room, I find a pair of tactical boots that belong to Mac and the leather battle vest that goes over Lark's head and straps around her ribs to compensate for her wings.

"Right, Flash mentioned we had a suite within Amberloq Hall."

Deciding to explore, I wander through the living area and poke my head into the next room.

Ah, the main bedchamber.

My feet are silent, cushioned by the plush pile of the carpet in this area. I'm not sure why I feel like I'm intruding. I live here too... don't I?

After my fight with Lark, I'm not so sure.

What would happen if Lark wanted me out of her life? Would Flash follow me or her? I don't even want to think about that. I haven't always been the most considerate of Flash, but he's my brother.

He'd choose me. Wouldn't he?

Maybe.

I think.

In all honesty, I'm not sure he would.

I rub at the hollow ache radiating from my chest. Everything is changing. It used to be my brothers and me against the world. Now they have their own lives outside of the three of us.

They have their own people to love.

JL MADORE

Once again, I feel like I've been left behind because I was judged and found lacking.

But whose fault is that?

I'd like to say the voice in my head was Shift laying into me, as he so often does. It wasn't. That connection was severed and now I am more alone than I have ever been.

Do Shift and Flash even miss my presence on our shared channel? The vulnerability of not knowing for sure lays me bare.

All my life, I've felt apart, separate from others. A single piece in a vast puzzle, always slightly misaligned. The only exception was my brothers. Our bond was my anchor in isolation.

And now that's gone.

I feel untethered, adrift. And knowing that the two of them are not only adapting but also excelling in this new life makes the hurt even more acute. The loneliness of my existence is amplified, echoing back at me in the silence of my thoughts.

"Link?"

I wipe under my eyes before turning toward the sound of Lark's voice. She meets my gaze, her radiance wavy behind the wall of emotion threatening to get away from me. "You came back."

She steps forward, taking in my state of distress. "Damn it, Link. Talk to me."

I open my mouth to tell her I'm fine, but instead of an excuse, the truth rushes out of me before I can stop it. "I feel so... alone," I admit, my voice barely above a whisper. "I've always felt separate. Now it's... it's just so much worse."

Her arms are around me in an instant, her cheek pressed against the muscle of my shoulder. I lean into her warmth and it's shocking how comforting it is. "You're not alone. I'm here. Not because I have to be or because I want anything from you. I chose to be your connection with this

96

world. I want to be here. So, get over yourself and let me in."

I close my eyes, grateful the universe chose such a warrior to be my catalyst. "I'm not an easy man."

She chuckles against me, her body jostling with her amusement. "I know who and what you are, and I'm still here."

Yes, she is... although a moment ago, she walked away. "I hurt you and I'm sorry."

"I shouldn't have slapped you."

"No. I deserved it. I regret the tears, though."

She eases back and meets my gaze. "Don't ever regret showing your pain. To see you cry proved to me that the man I know is in there truly *is* in there."

I swallow. "I meant your tears. I was deliberately cruel when you were trying to be kind. I'm sorry."

She nods and leans in for another tight embrace. "Apology accepted. Now, how about we get you downstairs and find you some food?"

"In a moment. If you don't mind, I'd like to stay here and hold you a little longer. Surprisingly, I find I enjoy having you all to myself."

She chuckles again. "Take all the time you need."

Shift

At the sound of a fight breaking out, I call my wings forward and launch straight into the air. My brother is in trouble and my pulse is thundering in my ears with the need to find him. The rooftop of the apartment building is long and flat and when I rise over the crest of the half wall, I see him.

The lion soldier.

The alpha feline enemy is here, and he's not alone. I tap the communication device in my ear. "Three soldiers. Apartment rooftop."

That's all the time I have before I'm charged, and the battle Flash is waging spills over on me.

Get down!

Flash's words echo in my head, and I drop to the ground and dive behind a metal stack without question. The *tat-tat-tat* of gunfire hitting metal behind me reminds me they have ammunition that takes us down.

In the last battle, I grabbed one of their guns and took them down instead.

Flash shouts and I roll to my feet. They aren't the only ones with guns. Gripping the phaser hanging across my chest, I vault straight into the air and target a fierce female about to round the corner of my hiding place and close in on me.

I fire two shots in quick succession, and she's knocked back. She almost goes over the low wall that borders the rooftop, but no such luck.

I catch sight of Flash throwing himself to the ground as the feline's claws swipe through the night air and narrowly miss him.

"Mac!" I call out, my heart pounding as a red Sith cat launches up the stairwell, his muscles rippling beneath his sleek coat. He leaps at the lion man, their snarls and roars filling the room.

I move to help, but I'm thrown back by a dark elf with a scar across his forehead. Dammit. "Flash, help Mac. I've got the elf."

Rolling to my feet, I scramble to get the phaser back into my hand. The dark elf doesn't give me the chance. He lunges forward, his twin swords glinting menacingly in the dim light.

I lurch back, barely getting out of reach, as the blades whistle past my head. As he comes at me again, Flash fires a shot toward us and hits one of the elf's hands. When he drops the sword, I retrieve it.

Now we're equally armed.

My thoughts race as I fight. *How is Mac? Is Flash watching over him?* I catch glimpses of them from the corner of my eye, their movements a blur of red fur and ebony mane.

My opponent seems to sense my distraction and presses his advantage. He comes at me like a whirling cyclone, forcing me back on the defensive. I refuse to be overwhelmed.

I parry his blows and search for an opening, waiting for an opportunity to strike.

Mac's cat lets off a vicious snarl, followed by a roar from his feline foe.

"On your left," Tundra says, swooping into the fray. The ivory winged Elbirfae targets the elf coming at me and twists the moment before they collide, his wing taking the brunt of the attack.

The sword does no damage.

Elbirfae wings are naturally armored.

The genius of nature.

Blue bolts of magic hit the elf as Dune drops Lukas gently to his feet. They affectionately call him Magic Man, but he's much more impressive than that sounds. "Can't let you boys have all the fun, now can we?"

The tides of the battle have turned, and everyone on this rooftop knows it. Six against three is more than enough to take them down now that we know how they fight and what their weaknesses are.

The dark elf staggers back, blood pouring from the wound Lukas' energy bolt caused. He glares with rage-filled eyes, and I shift closer to Lukas to cut off any idea of retaliation.

Lukas is formidable, but he's still just a human male. He doesn't have the durability we do.

"Give it up, boys," Lukas says, his voice cold and unyielding. "Brass is a sinking ship. He's got you all twisted up. You're fighting for the wrong team."

Dune has joined Mac and the two of them are taking down the woman. She's bleeding almost as bad as the dark elf and is moments away from being shut down altogether.

The lion warrior is losing ground and we all know it. He sees the loss gaining on him and his gaze darts around, searching for an exit strategy.

"There's nowhere to go, cousin," I say, leaving Lukas and Tundra to deal with the elf. "Andras Brass is using you. We were created to serve the Amberloq and be warriors for the Crown of Dornte. He stole that from you. He's using you as his personal army."

The lion man roars. "Lies. You are the enemy. You turned on our maker and have no honor."

Flash laughs. "How did we turn on our maker? He woke us from stasis and left us to die in that bunker. We didn't rank high enough for him to take us. He doesn't care about us."

"You," he shouts. "He might not care about *you*, but he cares about *us*."

I shake my head. "Your brothers and sisters are programmed to terminate when captured. How is that caring? We are strong enough and strategic enough to work our way through almost any scenario, yet he'd rather see us dead than in the hands of the people who commissioned our construction. Why do you think that is?"

A long, low growl is the only response I get.

Without warning and without giving us a chance to stop him, the feline folk alpha lion launches off the roof and disappears from sight.

"Shit," Lukas races to the edge, followed by Tundra and Dune, who continue past the wall and throw themselves into the air. As they sink below our line of vision, their wings flare and I know this will be one hell of a chase.

"I want that," I say to Flash.

"You want what, brother?"

"The three of them work so well as a team they don't even have to voice their commands. They simply act as a unit. I want to have that with you, Link, Lark, and Mac."

Lukas straightens and turns to meet us with a smile. "You'll get there. It just takes time and trust."

"That leaves Link out," Flash says.

I sigh. "Yes, sadly, it likely does."

CHAPTER THIRTEEN

Mac

$\mathcal{A}$fter the battle, Dune, Lukas, and Tundra secure the woman and the dark elf and load them into their SUV. They need medical help to patch them up and then Tundra will probably rip them apart again, trying to find out where Yarko, Skye, and Beta are being held.

Tundra is already in a foul mood about losing the lion man in the chaos of the city streets. I don't think it will take much more to bring him to violence.

When we park the truck, we say goodnight and begin the forest trek back to Amberloq Hall. I'm always wired after my cat lets loose in battle, but tonight, I'm especially wound up.

Watching Shift and Flash in action is such a fucking turn on. The precision of their moves. The strength in their stance.

They are warrior porn.

"And what if we learn nothing from them?" Flash asks. "How will we find Beta and the kids if no one will tell us where they're being held?"

I'm having trouble focusing on small talk, but we're still too far away from our private space to lose control now. "Odds are, Brass has them. We find him, we'll find them, too."

The faint crackle of leaves to our left accompanies other people out for a walk in the moonlight of the castle grounds. Now is not the time or place to ravage these two.

No matter how much I want to.

"It's heartening that everyone is dedicated to finding them," Shift says. "They barely know Beta, and from what Skye said, she and Yarko are simply orphans that landed on Lark and Tundra's doorstep."

I chuckle. "It's called found family. We're not just soldiers here, lads. We're part of a team—a family. If there's one thing ye'll learn about us, it's that we don't leave family behind."

Shift slides his palm against mine and laces our fingers. "We're honored to be included in your lives."

Flash sighs and kicks a rock up the path ahead of us. "Now, if we can only teach Link what it means to be part of a family."

"He knows what it means," Shift says. "He just doesn't trust it. He'll come around. We have to give him time."

Shift has a lot more faith in their autocratic third than I do. From what Link has shown me, he's all about himself, his ambitions, and his needs.

I hope I'm wrong, but I'm usually not.

As we near the end of the path, I bring Shift's hand to the adrenaline erection I've been sporting for the past half hour. "It's good to be home."

Shift chuckles. "Having a solid erection after a highly charged event is perfectly normal. It's simply an excess of adrenaline and testosterone put to good use."

"I thought I was the only one," Flash says, rubbing a caressing hand over the front of his pants.

I laugh. "Hardly. Why do you think warriors are considered such virile beasts? It's because we come off the battlefield and want nothing more than to ravage our partners."

"That's my plan," Flash says. "The moment we're in our suite, I'm stripping down and sticking my cock somewhere warm and wet."

I snort. "Just anywhere?"

Flash grins. "Anywhere it's welcome."

Too funny. "Well, yer in luck because as soon as we find Lark—"

"You're in luck," Lark says, jogging down the steps off the back deck, hand-in-hand with Link. "You found me. What did you want me for?"

"Much sex," Flash says, rushing forward and lifting her off her feet to hug her.

I give Lark credit. She takes the frontal assault in good humor, meeting Flash's kiss with equal fervor before pulling back.

All the while, she's still holding Link's hand.

Something shifted while we were away, and I'm not the only one who notices.

"Where are you two off to?" Shift asks, voicing our shared curiosity.

Lark turns her head to face the breeze and moves a lock of wayward hair out of the way. "I'm taking Link to soak in the milk baths. Honor told me the medicinal benefits are long praised as one reason Amberloq warriors seem indestructible. She says their regenerative power might even rival Calli's phoenix tears."

"That's a big claim," I say.

She looks at me and her brow pinches. Then she takes in Flash and Shift. "You've been in a battle. Are you all right?"

"Fine, lass," I assure her.

"Did you find the Gen-3s? Did you find Brass?"

I shake my head. "No. We tracked down where they've been buying one of the rare components for the serum and ran into three of them."

"We won the battle and captured two more," Flash says. "And now we have mighty battle cocks from all the adrenaline and testosterone."

Lark blinks and then searches our faces. "All of you do?"

I waggle my brows at her. "Afraid so. I hope yer not sore from this mornin', lass, because yer males are back from battle and we're hungry."

Lark pulls Link back into motion and points to the low bungalow building around the other side of the pond. "Then you should join us. I'm sure your muscles could use a little battle aftercare. And then we can see what to do about your battle cocks."

"And we'd like to hear what transpired tonight," Link adds.

We relay the night's events as we cross the grounds. Flash tells most of it. He's in a good mood and is animated and excited to tell Lark all about it.

He's a lot like a sweet puppy.

Spending time with Flash is like wrapping yourself in joy.

"—and if they have any luck with the interrogations, we might have intel about Beta and the kids by morning," he says.

"The Gen-3s won't talk," Link says.

Flash's face falls. "They might. Lukas tried to tell them they're fighting for the wrong side. Between Josie and the scientists, they might clean up Brass' programming and set them straight."

I expect Link to argue and kick our little puppy, but he doesn't. He seems to check his instinct and take another tack. "Perhaps you're right. I suppose we'll have to wait and see."

Flash smiles and grabs the door, holding it open so the rest of us can pass. He misses Lark hugging Link's arm and kissing his cheek.

Yes, something definitely shifted between these two tonight. Maybe Link's come back from his moment of reckoning as a changed man.

Wouldn't that be nice?

~

Lark

The bathing area is a long, rectangular room with eight sunken troughs in the floor. The milky water that fills them is heated by a natural spring that runs beneath the grounds. There is a decorative skylight overhead, but because it's well past the rise of the second moon, the only thing we see is the silver glow of the night sky.

"Flash, sweetie, lock the door," I say. "There's no reason to scar the kids if they wander over here tonight."

Flash is quick to do as I ask and then is pulling his shirt over his head and tossing it. Next go his fatigues and then he looks to me, waiting for an invitation.

Wow. As Shift and Mac both get undressed, the whole adrenaline hard-on issue comes into full focus.

Full. Frontal. Focus.

I swallow and rub my hand over my mouth to make sure I'm not drooling. Thankfully, I'm not, because that would be more than a little embarrassing.

"Go ahead," Links says, squeezing my hand before gesturing to the three. "Ease the heroes of the night. I'm going to soak for a bit and am happy to watch."

I meet his gaze and search for any sign that this is an empty offer. It's not. "But we were going to soak together."

"Like I said earlier, I'm looking forward to one-on-one time with you. It'll keep. We'll get there."

I'm torn. Tonight was supposed to be about making strides with Link, not me playing with the other three and leaving him out.

"No. You know what? Five in a relationship will only work if everyone gets what they need. Flash, sweetie, I had plans with Link. Can you occupy yourself with Shift and Mac for a bit?

Flash looks from me to Link and breaks out in the most glorious smile ever seen. "Of course, lovely. You two have fun."

When I look back to Link, there's no missing the shock in his golden gaze. "I meant what I said just now. For this to work, everyone must get what they need, and right now, I need time with you."

Before he argues or ruins the moment by opening his mouth, I take his hand and guide him down to the far end of the building.

After last night, I know Mac, Shift, and Flash can amuse themselves. And that's great because right now, I only have eyes for Link.

"Here, let me help you undress."

Link scoffs. "I'm not so badly off that I can't remove my clothing."

"In no way do I think you can't get undressed. I *want* to take off your clothes. I want to run my fingers across your chest and over your shoulders and down your hips. It's a form of affection and the two of us getting familiar with one another... unless you don't think of me like that."

I hesitate, worried that I read him wrong. "Oh, sorry. I offered you companionship and support and then I assumed we'd get to know each other better. If that's not..."

I step back, but he catches my wrist and moves to keep me close. "I told you before, I'm not good at this. I have the skills and programming to be a memorable lover, but we weren't designed to build relationships. If I miss a cue, it doesn't mean you're wrong, and it certainly doesn't mean I wish you to stop."

I let out a long breath and relax a little. "All right. Then, if you don't object, I'd like to help you out of your clothes and into the milk bath."

"I do not object." Link lets me have my fun without saying

another word. He lifts his arms when I tug his shirt over his head and his feet when I slide off his boots and socks. And he's silent as a chiseled statue as I slide his pants down the sculpted planes of his hips and thighs.

Utter perfection.

With him standing naked before me, my breath is shallow, my mouth is flooding with the need to swallow, and someone must've turned up the temperature of my inner furnace because I am about to overheat in several key parts of my body.

"You like what you see," Link says, his mouth curving up in a cocky smirk.

"Of course, I do. You're a beautifully made male. Now, would you like to undress me or watch me undress myself? Gentleman's choice."

"Let me," he says, a storm of emotions swirling in his warm, caramel colored gaze. "I want to become more familiar with you, too."

Link

Lark's body differs from mine. Obviously, she is a female and naturally born, but there are other differences I find even more fascinating. Her wings are heavy, not retractable, and branch out of her muscled shoulder blades. They emerge high on her back and almost act as another set of appendages.

Mine eject from the ridge on both sides of my spine and retract when not in use. They allow me to fly, but I can't bring them around my body and use them as a shield or to strike people as she can.

Standing behind her, I unfasten her shirt at both sides and lift the flap of fabric over her head. It drops to the tile floor of the bathing house with a whisper.

Sweeping her long hair to the side, I settle it over the front of her shoulder so I can continue my exploration. Her wings are powerful, graceful, and her ebony feathers are as soft as the most precious down.

"Flex your wings open for me."

She turns her head and smiles at me over her shoulder, slowly flexing her wings from their resting position down the length of her back and buttocks to unfurl to the sides.

"You say *I* am beautifully made, but there is nothing I have ever seen more beautiful than your warrior frame." I brush my fingers across the back of her shoulders and down the ridges of her spine. I caress the base of each wing, marveling at how the appendages hinge to her frame.

She shudders beneath my touch and lets off a soft, feminine gasp. "Just so you know, the base of a female's wings is an erogenous zone. You're welcome to keep stroking me there, but don't be surprised if I turn around and mount you."

I pause my exploration, not sure if I'm ready for the intimacy that might imply. "I'll keep that in mind. For now, I'm entranced with undressing you."

I move to her front and start my inventory at the top: long, silky black hair that shines blue in certain lights, piercing green eyes, a slender neck, strong shoulders... "Your breasts are lovely. I realize I already removed your shirt, but may I touch them?"

"You may."

I circle my finger around the fleshy mounds, first the one on the right and then the left. Then I cup my hand under the right and test its weight.

There have been a couple of heated moments when I have been invited into the passions of my brothers and have seen or sampled Lark's body, but nothing like this.

Tonight isn't about my brothers or being lost in the lust of bonding magic. This moment is about Lark trusting me with her body.

She's trusting me in the hopes I will trust her in return. I want to. I'm just uncertain it's wise for me to give any part of me away when my systems aren't functioning properly, and my judgement could be off.

I brush my thumb over her beaded nipple. "What makes the tips harden and protrude like this?"

"Cool temperatures or arousal."

With the baths being filled by hot springs, the temperature is balmy. So, arousal? Does she enjoy my touch?

Deciding to file that away for later, I frame her body in my hands and move down her ribs to her hips. Unfastening her pants, I ease them down her thighs, and then kneel before her to remove her shoes, and free her legs. That leaves her standing above me in only a slip of silk that hides her core from my view.

"And this?" I raise a finger to touch the fabric at the crux of her legs.

"What about it?"

"Do I have the honors of stripping you bare?"

"If you like."

I do. It seems ironic. She is a warrior who battles and fights and is strong, but there is another side to her. She is also delicate and smells of feminine musk.

This life we live is dangerous and I could lose any of them at any time. Why do I spend so much time being obstinate and pushing people away?

The ache of despair and loneliness returns. It's lucky I'm already kneeling because it hits with such power, it could take me to the ground.

Lark's hand rakes my scalp, her fingers lacing through my short hair. "Everything all right?"

Just that simple connection draws me back. I look up the length of her body and meet the concern in her gaze. "Not yet, but I'm trying."

Her smile is filled with more understanding than I ever

thought possible. She tugs me to my feet and wraps me in a hug. "You're doing great. I'd rather you be honest and take your time than rush and be twisted up in knots."

I ease back from her embrace. "Twisted up in knots is my default setting."

"Not anymore, surly man. I'm going to teach you how to unwind and start appreciating what's around you. Life is good. You'll see."

I hope she's right. Deep down, I want to believe her. I want there to be more to my life than bickering with my brothers and trying to keep them from branching out in the world.

"How can a genetically designed super soldier be so afraid of what comes next?"

She holds my cheeks in the palms of her hands and smiles. "Because as well as there being different kinds of intelligence, there are also different kinds of strengths. You enjoy controlling situations, but in real life, control is an illusion."

I grunt. "I thought you were trying to make me feel better."

Her grin and the soft giggle that escapes her throat are too cute. "Oh, I intend to make you feel amazing. Whether it's just the milk baths or something more takes hold, tonight is about you and whatever you need to find your footing."

I like the sound of that. "Then perhaps we can soak for a while together. If more comes of it, that's great. If not, I could use the time to relax and heal."

"That's an inspired idea." She shimmies off the cotton slip of underwear and tosses it toward the pile of discarded clothes. Then she lowers herself onto the edge of the closest bathing trough and eases into the milky bath.

The creamy white water envelopes her tanned skin and pools around the top of her breasts. As the surface adjusts, it exposes her peeked nipples in a playful game of hide and seek.

Lark swishes her arms in the liquid and floats toward the angled end of the trough that acts as a backrest. "Are you going to join me, or just stand there gawking with your cock bobbing in the air?"

I glance down and cup my erection. "I think these baths were intended for one person."

She waves that away. "Not tonight, they aren't. Come. Join me. I promise you won't regret it."

"Fine. I'll trust you." The words might seem simple, but the pledge behind them is not.

She seems to understand my full meaning and opens her arms to welcome me. The warmth of the water climbs up my legs, hips, and then chest. It may possess a miraculous power of healing... but no more so than my catalyst.

I meet Lark chest to chest and spin in the trough so my back is against the stone and she's cradled in my lap. "You know, I thought I might get in and not want to get out. Now I'm sure I won't. Are you prepared to stay with me for the duration?"

"I'm not going anywhere."

CHAPTER FOURTEEN

Lark

$\mathcal{T}$he morning after the night before is a delicate balance of trying to keep Link in a good place while not neglecting the others. It's early days, I understand that, but I get the feeling Link isn't really a fivesome kind of guy.

"What does that mean?" Flash whispers, pushing his plate away. "He can't have you all to himself all the time. Does he expect you to sleep in his room every night? We missed you last night."

"I missed you too, sweetie, but things with Link are fragile right now."

"But sleeping apart was supposed to be temporary."

I squeeze his thigh below the breakfast table and make sure our conversation is still private. "Don't panic. Link made significant progress yesterday. Let's give him a chance to let it all sink in."

Flash leans back in his chair and grunts. "You forget, lovely, we know Link better than you. If he's accepting you and not the complete package of all of us, he's planning to cut us out."

"No. I won't let that happen."

"Then you'll have to be prepared to hit him head on," Shift says, pausing with his coffee mug at his lips. "Flash is right. Once Link decides something, it's almost impossible to change his course."

I sigh, not sure how to handle that. "But he joined us before. He likes to watch."

"And that's fine," Shift says, "as long as he doesn't think he can monopolize you all the time."

A clatter of silverware and the sudden scraping of chairs against the floor jolt us from our conversation.

"Yarko? Where the hell have ye been, lad?" Mac asks, walking over from the stove. He abandons his plate on the counter and rushes toward the two. "Skye, are ye all right, lass?"

Skye's knees give out and Mac has her scooped up in his arms and is striding for the door. "Shift, yer with me. Flash, get Yarko to the livin' room. Lark, let people know."

The scramble of bodies is impressive as we all act at once. Dune, Tundra, and I worked out this morning, and then they had a session with the kids. After that, they retreated to their suite to shower and get cleaned up for the day.

Racing into the grand foyer, I launch straight up to the landing and run down the hall toward the grand suite for the Guardian of the Crown. When I get there, I bang my fist on the door with more energy than I intend to, but the adrenaline is pumping.

"Not a good time," Dune shouts inside.

I hate to interrupt them, but this can't be helped. "Yarko and Skye just appeared in the kitchen," I shout through the door. "Skye collapsed, so Shift is—"

The door swings wide and I have to jump back to keep from getting bowled over by Tundra pulling on a pair of boxers. "Where are they?"

"Living room," I say.

Lukas is out next. He at least has pulled on a pair of training pants and is tying the waistband. Damn, Honor's mates are in fine shape. "He flashed them home? Does he know where they were?"

"We didn't get that far," I say, rushing down the hall, following him. "They just appeared."

I opt to take the stairs down with Lukas instead of flying down in case he has more questions. We only get halfway down the first flight when Moonshade comes racing past us, her tail wagging.

"This isn't a game, sweet girl," Lukas says, gripping the railing to keep from getting knocked down the stairs.

"Or maybe it is," I say, chuckling as she turns around and takes another run at tripping us.

Remarkably, the three of us make it to the bottom without injury, and Dune lands beside us at the base of the stairs. "Were they injured?"

"They didn't seem to be," I say, trying to think. "They were literally in front of us for ten seconds before Skye collapsed and we all scattered. It's hard to say what shape they're in."

By the time we make it to the living room, there is a crowd to push through. The trainees were obviously closer than Tundra and the others in their suite.

"Back it up, kids," Lukas says, striding through the sea of Elbirfae friends. "Well, now. It's good to see you, buddy."

Yarko is sitting in one of the oversized chairs, looking dazed and rather green.

"Watch the splash zone," River says, pointing to the waste bin in Yarko's hands. "He said they've been keeping him drugged. Seems like his body is done with that now."

As if to prove River's point, Yarko doubles forward and retches. The sound of vomit splashing into the bottom of the bin is gross enough. Having that accompanied by at least two other kids gagging is enough to start a chain reaction.

I wave my hands toward the doorway. "Okay, kids, give us ten minutes to sort things out. Go outside or wait in the other room or something. We'll fill you in as soon as we know what happened."

There are a lot of teen grumblings, but they file out and leave us to tend to our two lost souls.

Link ends up pushing against the flow of traffic to join us and I'm surprised to see the relief in his eyes when he sees Shift working on Skye. "Is she all right?"

"She will be," Shift says, straightening and moving to Yarko next. "She's been dosed with some kind of paralytic agent. It's wearing off, but it's left her quite dehydrated. Perhaps a bottle or two of those sport drinks the kids chug down like water."

"On it," Mac says, hustling to the doorway. "Someone bring us four bottles of electrolyte water."

"What flavors?" Bay calls back.

"That's neither here nor there, lad. Just bring them."

There's a scramble out in the hall and Mac is chuckling as he comes back to join us. "Are ye up to tellin' us what happened, son?"

Yarko leans back against the cushion of his chair. "We got jumped during the trials," he says, his voice raw and a little slurred. "Some of the trial applicants... they knocked us out. We woke up in a room... They forced pills on me that kept me from traveling."

Lukas nods. "We figured as much. They didn't want you to offer us a chance to evacuate."

"Everything is foggy after that," he says, reaching up to accept the bottle of liquid being offered to him. "Then this morning I started puking. The more I did, the less like a zombie I felt."

"He has food poisoning," Shift says, finishing with his exam. "It doesn't seem intentional. Likely food they gave them sat too long."

Yarko scoffs. "Zombies don't have much of an appetite. Yeah, our food usually sat for a while."

"What about Beta?" Flash asks. "Did you see Beta when you were a prisoner?"

He shakes his head. "No. Sorry."

The disappointment on Flash's face is mirrored in the expression of others in the room. There's nothing to be done about that.

"Here she comes," Link says, hanging over the back of the couch, watching Skye. "Welcome back, little one."

Tundra is sitting on the edge of the sofa and pulls her up into a hug. "Thank the powers you're all right. I was losing my mind."

"Too. Much. Love." Skye's breathy words have Tundra easing back and releasing her.

"Doc is coming," Honor says, joining us. "And Keyla is spreading the word to everyone who's been on standby, worrying."

Yarko hands me his drink with an urgency that tells me he's about to have another run of vomiting.

"Would you be more comfortable in a bathroom somewhere?"

He shakes his head. "No. I'd like to stay with all of you. I might need a fresh bucket though."

Mac meets Bay's gaze, and the kid is off and running again. "On it."

Yarko groans as all the fluid he just swallowed comes back up. "I feel like ass."

I squeeze Yarko's shoulder. "The important thing is you're home. Everything else we can deal with."

Mac

Doc gives Yarko a shot to slow the barfing a little and then Lukas asks him what we're all waiting to hear. "Do you think you could portal us back there?"

Yarko looks ill, but I don't think it has anything to do with his bout of food poisoning. "You need me to say yes, don't you?"

Lukas shrugs. "It would be our best chance to track down Brass and his network of followers and put an end to it, but if you can't, just say so."

He closes his eyes and deflates. "Can't isn't the same as not wanting to."

I squeeze the kid's shoulder. "Not wantin' to go back there is understandable, son. We're not askin' ye to stay. If ye could just place us wherever yer captives had ye, we'll take care of the ride home."

"Just a drop off?" Yarko asks, his spirits lifted.

"Aye. Just a quick in and out."

Everyone in the room stills, nonchalantly waiting for his answer. Inside, we are all dying to get going. "Yeah. I can do that. Give me two minutes to freshen up and then I'll take you."

The moment he stands, he lists to the side, and everyone scrambles to catch him.

"Whoa, who spun the world on me there?"

Lukas meets Dune's gaze and then tilts his head toward the hall. Dune rushes in and gathers Yarko to his side. "Hey, buddy. How about I escort you to the bathroom and make sure you don't take a header?"

When they are out of the room and shuffling down the hall, Lukas frowns and looks to Doc and Shift. "Are we asking too much for him to portal us? Will it put him in danger?"

Neither of them looks sure.

It's Shift who speaks. "Portaling consumes energy. The boy has been drugged, poisoned, and has been vomiting for hours. There's no way of knowing what the expenditure of energy might cost him."

"But he'll bounce back, right?" Flash asks. "Lark's always saying how resilient the kids are. He can take us and then rest for a month. At least then we'll have a shot at catching Brass."

"But at what cost?" Lark asks.

Doc sighs. "Yarko isn't an ordinary kid. He's got warrior in him—has had his whole life. He's survived a lot over the past few years. He's tough."

"What if he gets you there and then can't get back?" Skye asks from the couch.

I scrub my hand over my face and exhale. "Aye, that's another problem all together, isn't it?"

"We could try Phoenix tears on him," Doc suggests. "We've only ever used them for healing injury, but they might be the cure-all he needs to get back on his feet."

Lukas nods. "Do it. Get him a vial of Calli's tears and then he can rest for the time we take to gear up and get ready."

"Will that be enough to ensure he's all right?" Lark asks.

Lukas shrugs. "I think so. If not, we shift gears and get him out of there ourselves. There's no way he ends up stuck as their prisoner again."

There's a grunt of agreement and it's unanimous.

Yarko comes first.

As he should.

CHAPTER FIFTEEN

Flash

The windowless room Yarko flashes us into is a depressing box with a bare mattress in the corner and a door to a basic powder room. For almost a week, these were the only four walls they saw.

Someone has to pay for that.

How is it that Brass and his power crowd think they get to treat people this way?

Is it money? Delusion? Do they honestly think themselves better than others?

Yes. Yes, they do.

Thankfully, the moment we're settled here, Yarko gives us a nod, and he flashes out. A moment later, Lukas gets a ping on his tactical watch, and he nods.

Yarko made it home safe.

With everything going to plan, it's time to find Brass and tear his world apart.

Mac makes quick work of the door and then Tundra, Dune,

and Lukas move silently up the corridor. Honor, Lark, and Mac follow, and then Shift, Link, and I take up the rear.

None of us are happy Link demanded to come, but we can't very well bench him from active duty when he's got the most invested in finding Brass and his scientists.

Besides, treating him like he's defective will just bring up all the wounds he's still picking at from when we were deemed unworthy and put into stasis.

As we make our way through the compound, the sun casts long shadows over the roofline of the building. It gives us an idea of the size and layout of the structure ahead.

It's a sprawling fortress, complete with high walls and watchtowers. A thick metal gate bars the entrance down the driveway and I have no doubt the entire property is rigged with security cameras searching for any signs of intruders.

But the intruders are already inside.

One by one, in silent precision, we clear the rooms on this floor. Eventually, we end up at the bottom of a stairwell. Everyone holds still for a moment and Mac and Shift move to listen at the base of the stairs.

After a moment, they shake their heads.

Whoever was holding Yarko and Skye hostage either haven't realized the kids escaped, or they have and have already evacuated.

On Lukas' order, our three teams creep up the stairs and expand our search. If Beta's here, we'll find him. *We're coming for you, brother.*

At the top of the stairs, Lukas signals for Honor, Mac, and Lark to continue to the next floor above. He, Dune, and Tundra take the main floor left, and he signals for us to take the main floor right.

The mansion sprawls off before us, imposing in its grandeur. Gold gilded portraits and crystal chandeliers and a hundred exorbitant ways to waste money on every square foot we pass through.

Our steps remain a ghostly whisper against the marble floor. Room by room, we continue our search, each dead end dropping another stone of disappointment into the pit of my stomach.

Beta has to be here.

Where else could he be?

We continue onwards, my mind racing with every step. Suddenly, I freeze. The almost imperceptible sound of movement catches my attention outside.

"Go," Shift says, covering the hallway.

I take the opportunity and hustle over to look outside. I don't see anything on the ground, but with the sun at its zenith, a dozen shadow Xs are floating across the grass.

What are those shadows coming from?

Then it hits me.

"Drones. We've got incoming!"

I barely get the words out when the whir of rotors grows louder. The electronic hum is like a swarm of mechanized bees. The hairs on the back of my neck prickle. We're about to be overrun.

"Shit," I hiss, launching myself from the window as they shoot out the glass and zoom inside. I'm running in a crouch, searching for a defensible position. "We have a situation! We're pinned down."

"Coming your way," Lukas' voice echoes over the comms. "Hang on. Everyone to the ground floor."

There's one terrible, deafening moment when everything stills. And then, chaos reigns.

More drones smash through the windowpanes around the main floor, glass exploding inward in a lethal rain. Link, Shift, and I shield our faces as shards of glass threaten to impale us.

The drones zip in, rotors a furious buzz, red targeting lasers dancing over the walls and doors, seeking us out.

As one laser finds me, I dive out of the beam.

Scrambling to my feet, I grip the phaser slung across my chest and return fire. The little monster machines have an incredible reaction time because they twist and toggle out of the way.

Lukas and Dune fire from the entrance of the kitchen. More drones pour in through the broken windows, seemingly annoyed that we'd dare to defend ourselves.

They're firing wildly.

"It's like a feckin' laser light show," Mac says, joining the fun.

"Ow, slecking hell!" Dune shouts, twisting behind the corner to avoid an incoming strike. "I hate these things."

"What do we do?" Lark yells.

We're outnumbered, trapped in a room rapidly filling with flying death.

"Adapt and adjust," Link shouts, his voice barely audible over the whirring drone blades and ceaseless gunfire. "We have the mathematical capability to assess their movement patterns."

"Do it and take them out of the air," Lukas shouts.

Link's right. It's not so different from the simulation calculations Brass used to have us do.

There are just more of them.

"I'll take the ones by the window," I say. "Link, you take the ones by the fireplace. Shift, you've got the ones pinning Mac and Lark in the stairwell."

"Do you need anything from us?" Dune shouts.

"You could distract them for us," I suggest.

"Anything other than that?"

Mac chuckles on the stairs. "Oh, come now, Sand Man. Yer a big strong Elbirfae. Get yer wings up and show these remote-controlled death machines who's boss."

I ignore them and throw myself back into my calculations. "Okay, Dune, now."

When Dune dive rolls through the air, several of the drones turn. I calculate their rotation as they adjust their gimble and recalculate their aim.

Pew. Pew.

Two drones hit the marble floor and Dune takes up a defensive position near the kitchen entrance. "Two down. A hundred to go."

Another round of shots goes off and Dune shields himself with his wings. "Slecking hell. Kill these stupid things."

I laugh, taking aim and recalculating to fire again.

Link and Shift are doing the same and one by one, our attackers are exploding mid-air.

Tundra decides to take a few hits for the team and comes out of his cover position. He fires upon them but doesn't hit any.

Link fires twice but doesn't hit his mark.

Shift takes out the ones targeting him, the downed unit taking out a couple of its compatriots in a shower of sparks and smoke.

"We haven't got the time or the power cartridges to play this game all day," Honor shouts from the stairs. "Call Yarko back. We need an exfil."

"What about Beta?" I shout. "We need to finish our search. He could still be here."

"I'm sorry, blondie," Mac says from across the room. "These drones were set up to take us out. They knew we were comin', lad. That means they knew the kids escaped and would be bringin' us here. If Beta was here, he isn't now."

I want to argue, but his logic is sound. "Fine. Call Yarko. We're done here."

～

Lark

Back in the Amberloq Hall kitchen, the energy is thick with tension and irritation. We got out, but not unscathed. The drones did their damage. We were caught off guard, and that stings more than the burns from the laser attacks.

The moment we materialize, Link slides his phaser onto the counter and balls his hands into fists. He's seething. I'm angry too, but he is next level pissed off.

"Link, did I miss something?" I scan the faces of the others but get no sense of what's upsetting him. "Are you all right?"

Link frowns. "No. I'm not. We just lost another battle against Brass and his forces."

"All is not lost, folks." Lukas holds up two drones we salvaged. "With these, we might trace the signal from the operators and expose another piece of the Brass puzzle.

I hope that's true, but I've never been good with tech... unless you count my relationships to the three.

"I'd like to work with one too," Link says. "If you'll trust me to take it and see what I can do."

Lukas looks surprised, but nods as he hands one of them over. "Your input and expertise are welcome. Thanks, Link."

"We can help," Shift says, gesturing to himself and Flash. "We were thinking if we can interface with the drone's port system, we might track where things come from easily."

Mac frowns. "And Brass and his people know that. If ye find an address that easily, I'd be surprised if it's not a trap."

Flash shrugs. "Whatever it takes to close the gap between us and Beta."

I grip Flash's wrist and give him a squeeze. "Sweetie. I know you want to find Beta functioning and well, and simply incapacitated somewhere, but Brass is crueler than that."

Flash meets my gaze, the sad reality reflected in his eyes. "I'm not under any false illusions, lovely. I know the deplorable depths of that man's cruelty. But I also know Beta wasn't at the mountain lodge after the explosion and he wasn't with Yarko and Skye. He has him and one day soon, we're going to figure out why."

"I believe that too." I just think it'll be something awful and don't want my guys torn up over it.

Mac seems to catch the subtext of my concerns and gives me an almost imperceptible shake of his head.

I think Link picks up on it too, but changes the subject before it gets too heavy. "Come, brothers. We have work to do."

When they leave, Doc joins us. "Anyone need a little TLC?"

Mac shakes his head. "A few scuffs and laser burns, but we managed. How are the kids?"

"Better. Skye ate some soup and is sleeping in her room and Yarko is laying on the couch with an IV and a bucket."

"He's still not keeping anything down?" I ask.

"Not much. But the good news is there's nothing diabolical about it. It's just garden variety food poisoning."

Dune pulls a bunch of beers from the fridge and starts handing them out. "It's ironic, don't you think? Here we are, scouring the quadrant for the two of them, and Brass' plan is foiled by bad tuna and Yarko throwing up the sedation tablets."

Tundra accepts a bottle and holds it up for a toast. "I'll take the win and won't complain."

I meet his bottle with my own. "Same."

Mac chuckles and opens his bottle. "Aye, sometimes the most incredible twists in a plan come from something utterly unexpected."

Tundra takes a long drink of his beer and leans back on the edge of the counter. "Honor mentioned the two of you spoke briefly about finishing the trials after Skye and Yarko were found, and the Brass issues were completed."

I take a sip of my ale and let the icy chill wind its way down my esophagus and into my belly. "We did. Obviously, the

Amberloq needs to rebuild its forces. We've got a great core of candidates here who are dedicated to the cause."

Dune nods. "You did amazing work with the kids. They are a pleasure to train."

I shrug. "I can't take all the credit. We had some special members of our community trapped in that goblin camp. They taught all of us how to fight."

"True," Lukas says, "but you taught them how to survive. That's an incredibly important skill. Those kids are well-adjusted, motivated, and focused on all the right things. That was definitely you."

"And they'll be great Amberloq," Dune adds.

I raise my bottle. "I think so too."

"And though not all the trainees stayed after the bombing," Mac says. "The ones who did will make fine additions as well."

Agreed. "So, are you thinking we should continue the training and the trials here on the castle grounds?"

Dune checks with the others, and everyone seems to agree. "Yeah."

"The kids will be thrilled. When are you thinking we start?" I ask.

Tundra glances around and then shrugs. "Tomorrow? We've already been doing morning training, so we'll just ramp it up."

"And if we get news of Brass?" I ask.

Lukas shakes his head. "Amberloq duties will always take precedence."

I think about it for a moment and nod. "Yeah, that sounds good. We'll start first thing tomorrow."

CHAPTER SIXTEEN

Lark

As the sun graces the morning sky, Amberloq Hall is washed with its golden rays. Tundra and Dune have just finished the final touches on the training course and it's my honor to get things started.

The trainees are gathered in front of me, both the Elbirfae teens and the applicants who stuck with us after the devastation of the Hekko Lodge bombings. Their bodies are taut with anticipation, and their eyes reflect the same determination I feel burning in my chest every time I'm out there serving the quadrant.

I raise my hands for silence, and the chatter among the trainees quiets down. "Good morning, everyone. It's a new day. A fresh start. And it's time to get back on track. Today we want to test your mettle. Not just your strength, speed, or agility, but also your endurance, determination, and your ability to adapt and think on your feet. This is what it means to be a soldier."

I pause, my gaze sweeping over each of them. "The course winds around the back of the pond, bringing you into a full circuit of challenges to make your way back to the finish line. It comprises five centers: weapons proficiency, combat matches, obstacle relays, rock climbing, and problem solving."

I gesture to the starting point of the obstacle course. "Your task is to work through each center, complete each challenge in the fastest time possible, and show proficiency and adaptability. You will be timed, but remember, the aim isn't just about speed. It's about technique, strategy, and teamwork."

A ripple of nervous energy courses through the group, but there is determination and commitment there, too. "I believe in each of you. You made it this far. Now let's see what you're truly capable of. Questions?"

River raises his hand. "Do we have to do them in order? With this many of us, can we spread out?"

"Absolutely. There are five centers. Just make sure you get to all five and you're good. Any other questions?"

"What about Yarko?" Dusty asks. "He's still good, right? He's not disqualified or anything because he's not out here?"

"Oh, no. Of course not. When he's feeling better, we'll run him through the course one on one and he'll get his chance. Don't worry about that."

That answer inspires a lot of relieved smiles and head bobs. I spoke about teamwork, but I think they've all got that one down already.

When no one else raises a question, I step over to the timing machine. "When you step past here, your time will be recorded. Each center has one, too. The chip we gave you in your arm band will track your arrival and departure from each center."

Several of the kids adjust their arm bands and nod.

"On my mark, we begin. Three, two, one... go!"

Mac

While Lark, Shift, and Flash are outside working the trial stations with Dune, Tundra, and Lukas, I spend the morning in the Amberloq war room with Link. Our security center isn't as big as the one at the castle, but it connects to all the same systems and it's in our home.

Working in my t-shirt and sweats instead of dressing for the royals at the castle is a win-win.

Perched on the edge of the table, my attention is focused on the drone parts scattered across the surface. Who knew something so small could have so many components?

Link's fingers dance over the metal, his eyes glazed as his consciousness interfaces with the machine's.

"Anything?" I ask, my voice cutting through the room's quiet hum.

Link's brow furrows, his fingers twitching slightly as he navigates the drone's systems. "It's a complicated process," he admits. "Nothing about tracking the signal is straightforward."

Of course not.

We're counting on these drones to provide a lead and give us a direction in tracking down Brass.

Of course, things couldn't be that simple.

"Can ye do that and have a conversation on another matter without losin' focus?"

Link's eyes flash to mine, a hint of frustration seeping through his otherwise calm demeanor. "Yes. I can compartmentalize tasks and run several streams of attention at one time. What is it you want to have a conversation about?"

I consider how I want to broach the subject and figure he's all about bold and brash, so I go that route. "I don't have any interest in the two of us fuckin' around, and I think ye feel the same."

Link pauses his work and gives me his undivided attention. Apparently, compartmentalizing aside, this demands his full attention. "I do."

"And whether ye go that route with Shift and Flash is none of my business."

"No. I'm not interested in that, either. They are my brothers."

"Fine, but they're both twisted up about ye tryin' to shut them out of Lark's bed."

He straightens, his gaze narrowing. "What are you trying to say?"

"I'm sayin', that if ye only have designs on Lark but want to watch the rest of us and enjoy yerself from the sidelines, that's fine, but ye'll not be takin' her into the spare room every night to sleep away from us."

A coy smile quirks up at the corner of his mouth. "And you speak for the three of them now, do you?"

"Not exactly, but we spoke and we're all in agreement."

Link folds his arms across his chest. "And what is the consensus?"

"That yer part of the five of us. Yer in this with us and we want ye to take part. We think ye should sleep in the big bed with us. Ye can keep to Lark, ye can have yer private moments, but she's not yers simply because ye chose one lover instead of multiple."

One thing about Link is that if he doesn't want to telegraph his emotions, he can drop a mask of indifference and you can't get a damn read on him if your life depends on it.

"And the four of you had this conversation?"

I dip my chin. "We're still workin' out what our relationships are, but we all agree ye need to be there with all of us and not just Lark."

After a long while, he dips his chin. "I will consider your points. Now, let us get back to work."

It isn't a request so much as a dismissal of the subject. Fine. I had my say.

Nodding, I lean back, and we lapse into silence, Link's fingers dancing and his mind hard at work.

Outside, the trials are well underway. Our mates are over-seeing the trainees as they battle obstacles, jockey for power, and work on securing the future they so desperately want to claim.

Here we are, the two of us, in the same battle.

He might not have liked what I had to say, but he heard me out and he knows where we stand. We are a quint and however the sexcapades play out, there are five of us in this relationship.

No one is more or less important than another.

I watch Link work, thinking about how that might play out in the future. When his body tenses, I straighten. "Are ye onto somethin'?"

He frowns and grows quieter still. Anticipation has my cat prowling to the fore.

He found something.

Why won't he tell me what it is? It seems like forever as I wait for him to be ready to catch me up, but eventually, he grins, his eyes glinting with triumph. "I've got a location."

Link

My attempts to bring down the drones may have been unsuccessful, but I came back from the failure and followed the operation signal back to a location.

The moment we have that, Mac opens a live call with Rhylan up at the castle, so I can tell him what I found. "It's a shell company within another, within another, but when I untangled the web, I found eight different bank accounts tied to the network."

Rhylan's grin widens. "Tell me the names match up with some of the one percenters I've been stalking. I've wanted to shut them down and seize their funds so bad for so long."

Mac nods. "Well, I think today's the day, dragon. I sent ye the list. Ye should have it now."

Rhylan glances down at the table and laughs. "Hot damn, this is going to be like whacking a hornet's nest."

"How will you proceed?" I ask.

"We'll hit them where it hurts most. Their wallets. When we freeze their accounts, we cut off Brass' money supply. That'll force him to surface."

"What if they are loyal to him, regardless?" I ask.

Mac shakes his head. "No. Those rich bastards are all the same. They ride the wave of power until it crests and then they jump ship before they go down."

"Check it out." Rhylan projects holographic images into the air above his table, revealing various financial transactions between the wealthy citizens and the shell corporations. "These people are about to have a very bad day."

"If ye take them down, can ye be sure they won't come after Creed and the Thornebane rule?"

Rhylan waves that away. "We've got them dead to rights and with the new global currency taking hold, we control the money. They are about to learn not to fuck with the Thornebanes."

The three of us carry on. We search through financial records, real estate holdings, and other pieces of evidence that could lead us to who is hiding Brass and where.

"Uh-oh," Mac says a time later. "This wealthy asshole is funding not only the coup, but also the distribution of illegal weapons."

"Good to know," Rhylan says. "Send me that info, Mac. I'll start working up a case against them. What kind of weapons?"

"Looks like black market imports from the Human Realm."

"I thought we put an end to that."

"Apparently not."

Rhylan scans the holographic evidence before him and then

starts manipulating the data floating above his war table. "Too bad, so sad. I'm shutting you down, asshole."

Mac laughs. "Yer havin' more than yer share of fun at work today, aren't ye, dragon?"

Rhylan grins. "This morning a weapons distributor, this afternoon corrupt socialites. Life is good."

"Aye, it is," Mac says, clapping his hands together. "I'm always up for taking down bad guys."

I watch Mac work with Rhylan, the two of them going through the data and shutting down access to business accounts.

Sometimes being a warrior for the crown means battling with keystrokes and not swords.

That gives me some comfort. Maybe if my systems can't be recalibrated, I'll still provide some use.

As we weave through a web of corruption and deceit, I can't help but feel grateful for the opportunity to be part of Brass' downfall.

So far, we're only taking down his support network, but we'll get to him—one frozen bank account at a time.

I watch the data stream as the endless list of transactions rise in the holographic field of our screen. My systems trig into a repeating occurrence and then a pattern emerges. "One moment. I've found something hidden within the data streams."

Rhylan pauses and I pull up a visual of the transactions I'm talking about. "There's a pattern, a reoccurring signal hiding within the noise."

My fingers skim over the keyboard and, with a few taps, I manipulate the data and isolate it. When I pull up the lines of code for them to see, I feel a strange sense of camaraderie.

I point to the lines of data I'm interested in. "These transactions... they're set up in a recurring pattern. Every third Thursday of the month, a significant amount is moved."

Rhylan and Mac lean in to assess.

Rhylan lets off a murmur of acknowledgement. "Well spotted, Link. We have a scheduled payment. Now, the question is, to whom?"

I tap into the transaction, tracing it back to its source. A sense of satisfaction fills me as I navigate the complex web of financial transfers, routing numbers, and account details. It's different from the battlefield, but it's a fight, nonetheless.

"It's another shell account," I say. "But this one just made a large transfer to the chemical factory on the Fringe we discussed yesterday."

Rhylan frowns. "So, the day after we expose their serum shop in the city center, they transfer money to another distributor of that component. Coincidence? I think not."

"Brass must be desperate to get that component and make up his serum," Mac says.

"Nobody wants unstable Gen-3 soldiers hanging around. That sounds dangerous."

"And yet he valued them more than my brothers and me," I say.

"His loss is our gain," Mac says. "Now, can ye trace the purchase back to the purchaser?"

I wade through the miasma of information. "It seems my Gen-3 cousins thought of that and have set up warding against my efforts."

"Can ye get through their blocks?" Rhylan asks.

"Possibly. I'll set up a program to funnel through the erroneous code and find us the information we're looking for. It'll take some time, but I believe we'll get what we need."

"When do you think it'll break through?"

I consider that. "Likely by early morning."

The dragon nods. "Brilliant. In the meantime, Dune, Tundra, and I can stretch our wings and visit the chemical factory in the Fringe."

"Do ye want us to come?" Mac asks.

He shakes his head. "No. You stay here and work on the trials. We need Amberloq. Great work, Link."

Despite the grimness of my situation, I smile. I may not be the super soldier I was designed to be, but I'm still a part of this. I'm still a warrior, and I can still fight... even if the battlefield has changed.

CHAPTER SEVENTEEN

Lark

My skin is still warm from the hot water as I towel off and pull on a pair of soft cotton shorts and a loose tank top. My hair is wrapped up in a towel and my body aches pleasantly from a day spent testing the limits of our new trainees. There's a sense of accomplishment in guiding them toward an amazing future, a feeling I wouldn't trade for anything.

Leaving the bathroom, I pad barefoot into the living area of our suite, ready to collapse onto the plush sofa with a glass of wine.

But as I round the corner, my footfalls stall and I'm stuck in the entryway. "What's going on here?"

The living room of our suite has been transformed. The furniture has been pushed aside to make room for... what looks like an impromptu dining set-up.

Our table is draped with a white tablecloth. There is soft lighting filtering in from strategically placed lamps, casting a warm glow on the room. The air is scented with the rich aroma of freshly cooked food, tantalizing my senses.

A soft chuckle draws my attention to my guys. Mac, Link, Flash, and Shift stand there, grinning at my surprise. Dressed in their comfortable attire, they look pleased with themselves.

"Well," Mac says, rubbing the back of his neck sheepishly. "Shift thought, since we're waiting until Link's program gives us an address, we might unwind a little with a little ice cream treat tonight."

Link nods, a stiff smile on his face. "Consider it our first indulgence as a committed unit."

His words seem simple, but they're not. Ever since he came back from spending the day with Mac, he's been preoccupied. It's more than his efforts to find Brass. Mac told me the two of them had a talk.

If he's considering us a 'committed unit', that talk must've got through to him on some level.

Shift strides over to me, gesturing to the table. "We asked the kids and rounded up some of your favorites. We've got three flavors of ice cream, berries, whipped cream, nuts, and gummy candies."

I'm touched by the gesture and thankful for a moment amid the training, the battles, and the endless struggles to just be alone with my guys and bask in our relationship.

I push up on my toes to kiss him, and he wraps his arms around me. Shift is a great kisser. I mean it to be a simple moment of affection, but as things usually do with him, our passions spark and things escalate quickly out of my control.

I groan as his hips grind forward, his hold on my ass rucking up the hem of my shorts.

"Look at that ass," Mac says, growling from over by the table.

"And just like that, I'm hard and ready to go." Flash chuckles.

"What about our ice cream treat?" I ask.

"Let it melt," Mac says. "I'm craving a whole different kind of indulgence right now."

Me too.

I cross the line of restraint, reaching down to palm the solid ridge filling out the front of Shift's pants. "I like melty ice cream too. Right now, I want to devour you boys."

"That works for me." Flash abandons the dishes on the buffet table and rushes over, peeling off his shirt in the next breath.

I practically rip Shift's pants open, my need to get to him undeniable. Shoving the fabric down his muscled thighs, I drop to my knees.

"It needn't be a one or the other situation," Mac says. "How about a bit of whipped cream and maybe a berry to sweeten the treat?"

Mac comes over with a spoon and a bowl filled with whipped cream. He dollops a spoonful onto the head of Shifts cock and then sets a plump purple berry into the white cream.

I take him in my mouth.

Shift arches back and his entire body shudders. I groan as I lick up the cream on his crown and work the fruity berry into my mouth. *So good.*

He grips the back of my hair, gently grinding against my mouth. "Oh, beautiful. Whatever you hunger for. Devour away."

"Ye look good gettin' sucked off, mate," Mac says, reaching over his head to pull his shirt off. "Is our little bird enjoin' her treat?"

"I hope so," Shift gasps. "She's doing that thing she does when the tip of her tongue splits the opening—"

I slide my tongue into the small slit at the top of his crown and flick at the opening.

"Yes, that!"

Mac lets off a long, seductive growl as he moves in behind me. Lifting my hips, he shoves my delicate shorts to the floor. "Spread yer feet, little bird."

His fingers slide down the crack of my ass and then he's playing in the moisture of my folds. I groan deep in my throat and Shift's cock jumps in my mouth.

"It doesn't take much to set our quint off on a sexual tangent," Flash says, chuckling.

"Not that you're complaining," Link says.

"Oh, no, that will never happen."

Shift grunts and leans back, catching himself on the doorframe.

Mac chuckles behind me, the pads of his fingers brushing over my clit. "A little weak in the knees, are you, soldier boy?"

"More than a little," Shift chokes.

I grip his sac and twist the delicate orbs as I suck him off. Having his length in my mouth as Mac's fingers slide inside me is sooo good.

"Make him come hard, little bird. Make his systems fritz."

"Twist his sac harder," Flash says, swallowing. "He can't speak right now, but he wants you to twist harder."

I chuckle around the length of his erection. I bet Brass didn't expect that use for telepathic communication channels when he designed these boys. I increase the pressure and play rougher with Shift's balls.

His hips convulse as his fingers grip the framework of the door. "Yes!"

Flash lies on the floor below me, reaching up to occupy himself with my breasts. "I've never played with them from this angle before."

Shift groans and then his hold in my hair tightens and his hips thrust forward. Warm streams of cum fill my mouth and I practically purr as I swallow him down. I love oral. Love giving it and love receiving it, so to start off by earning his orgasm is perfection.

The contrast between sweet and salty, warm and cool and creamy is delightful. I like dessert sex play.

When the waves of his release calm, Mac pulls me off Shift's cock and lifts me to straddle his hips. His mouth is hot and demanding on mine as he carries me to the table.

Setting me onto the tablecloth, he eases back from the kiss. "Did you enjoy your treat, little bird?"

I brush my finger against my lip, claiming every drop. "I did. Shift is delicious."

"Aye, he is." Mac winks. "Now lay back while the rest of us have our fun."

I do as I'm told and lie back. Flash moves to the table above me and tugs my top off so that I'm naked and laid out like an offering.

"I know what I want to feed on," Link says, opening my knees.

"Patience," Mac says, bringing over the bowls from the buffet. He sets them on the table on both sides of my ribs. "We need to play with our food before we eat her."

The three don't need much prompting because they all pick up bowls and start eyeing me up like a sundae buffet. "Do ye like chocolate, Link?"

Link dips his chin and accepts the bowl of ice cream. "I do."

Mac waggles his brow at me and then scoops a spoonful onto my navel. It's cold and melty and spills across the surface of my skin and down my hips. Then, he smears some with the back of the spoon onto the top of my mons.

"Shift, will ye dab some cream and berries there for me, mate?"

Shift takes a spoonful of whipped cream and slathers my folds before placing four berries across my pubic bone. "One for each of us. Who wants to go first?"

"I will," Link says. "Let's see if just a taste will sate my sweet tooth. I'm guessing it won't."

Shift and Flash watch with rapt interest, their heads tilted to the side like curious puppies as they do when they're considering new concepts.

Mac scoops a spoonful of black cherry ripple into his mouth and grins as he looks on. "Do ye like my little game, boys?"

Link has crawled up the table between my legs and is lapping at the ice cream, swiping his hot tongue through the cold treat.

I groan and my back arches off the table.

"Do ye want to play too, little bird?"

"Yes."

"Flash, why don't ye give our girl a gummy and then decorate her like a holiday cookie?"

Link draws his tongue up the length of my channel and delves into the warmth at my core.

I cry out as Flash leans over the table, his eyes alight with mischief. "Can I pick anywhere on her body?"

"Anywhere ye like," Mac says. "Although we all know where yer headed."

Flash isn't listening anymore. He's got his sights set on my breasts and he's spooning two large dollops of whipped cream before topping each mound with a candied gummy.

Mac chuckles. "What did I tell ye? Flash is a breast man to the end."

Splayed across the table with Link buried in my core, Flash smearing my chest with whipped cream and candy, and Shift coming at me with a bowl of his own—I'm in heaven.

Can this be real?

Can this be my life?

Mac comes around the table and leans over, a wicked smile gracing his handsome face. "Lift yer head fer me, luv."

"Why? What are you up to?"

He dangles a strip of black fabric and grins. "Yer about to be blindfolded and ravaged by yer four mates. Any objections?"

I swallow. "None."

"Good girl. Now, lay back and let us have our fun. I promise ye'll love it."

Shift

It's the middle of the night when I wake and realize Link isn't in bed with us. Mac told me about their conversation in the war room and when he joined us in our dinner feast and then the shower afterward, I thought we'd had a breakthrough with him.

Perhaps not.

Rounding the bed, I check to see if he simply needed the washroom. He's not there, so I cross the suite and peer into the spare room. He's not there either.

Normally, I'd just access our private communication channel and ask him where he is. For right now, that's not an option.

Heading back to our bedroom, I try to remember where my clothes were discarded. I lost my pants by the door. I think my shirt came off by the table…

I'm tracking my clothes down when movement on the training grounds catches my attention.

Magnifying my vision, I confirm its Link on the opposite side of the pond.

What are you doing, brother?

It doesn't take me long before I figure that out. He's running the trainee drills… and by the look of things, he's struggling.

"Everythin' all right, soldier boy?" Mac asks, sliding in behind me at the window.

I drop my clothes, turn from the window, and wrap my arms around his hips. I love Mac, but Link's pain is private. If he wanted to share it, he would. And until it affects someone else, it's his alone.

"Everything's fine. I was just about to come back to bed. Any chance you'll join me?"

Sleepy Mac is one of my favorite looks on him. He yawns, scrubs a hand over his face, and nods. "Lead the way."

CHAPTER EIGHTEEN

Flash

The three of us wake early and start our day before the sun rises. Link is hoping his tracking program has done its job and we'll have a lead on Brass. We walk to the castle and make our way to the locked door at the top of the stairs. It leads down to the security room where Rhylan works his magic.

Unfortunately, we don't have clearance to be down here ourselves, so the guard calls Rhylan and summons him from his suite. "Please, gods, tell me you at least brought me coffee."

The dragon is looking tired, and I worry his weary expression is because of his recent mission to the Fringe and not from the early hour or our empty hands. "Apologies. We do not drink coffee."

"I'm sad for you," he says, keying a code into the security pad beside the door. "You should start."

"We are eager to find out how your trip to the Fringe went last evening. Did you stop the purchase of the serum component?"

The door bangs against the wall as he lets us in. "No such

luck. The order had already been filled. Brass got his hands on the component for the serum, and the billing information on the file was fake."

Link curses. "So, we're back to nowhere with nothing to go on."

Rhylan points a finger at him. "Precisely. It seems the name of this game is 'Too Little, Too Late.'"

I grunt. "I want to play a different game for a while. One called 'We Have the Advantage, And We Win.'"

Rhylan turns on the war table and clicks on the monitors on the far wall. "I'm with you. Let me know when we can play that game instead."

Shift moves over to the war table and looks at the information materializing in the air. "Assuming Brass has what he needs to make his next batch of serum, now he won't have to surface anytime soon."

I grab a chair from the corner and take a seat. "Which might slow the Gen-3 attacks, but won't get us any closer to finding out what happened to Beta."

Link sighs. "And it doesn't get us any closer to finding his research and equipment, either."

Yeah. Poor Link. Shift told me he saw him training alone in the middle of the night to pull his life back together.

He's struggling with balance and coordination and obviously doesn't want us to know how bad it is.

A notification goes off on Rhylan's watch and he turns it over to read it. "Apparently, you three aren't the only early birds this morning. There's someone outside asking to see me. They say they have information I'll be interested in."

"Information about what?" Link asks. "Do you think it's about Brass or the Gen-3s?"

"Only one way to find out." Rhylan gestures toward the door, and we all file out into the hall. He locks things up again and then we're down the hall, up the stairs, and headed toward the staff entrance of the castle.

Anticipation builds in my chest with each step. Is it too much to hope that this unexpected visitor holds the key to unlocking our search for Andras Brass?

Easy, brother, Shift says into my mind. *We have no idea who is here or why.*

But they might have information.

And even if they do, it might not be legitimate.

I suppose that's true too.

As we approach the exit, the guard dips his chin and opens the door. Rhylan is the first one through and then Link, Shift, and me.

The moment we're outside, Rhylan stops dead in his tracks and his entire frame stiffens. "Well, on the list of people I least expected to be shadowing the castle doorstep, you'd be on the top."

I stare at the man mirroring Rhylan and wonder if my systems are malfunctioning like Link's. There are two of them… identical.

"Bloody hell," Lukas curses, coming out of the trees and joining us. "What the fuck are you doing here, dragon?"

I scan my diagnostics for inconsistencies. But everything checks out. There are indeed two Rhylans present. The one who arrived claims to have intel has long, golden hair that obscures much of his face where Rhylan's hair is shaved short on the sides and back and longer on the top.

"Nice to see you, too, asshole. Miss me?"

"Not even a little," Lukas replies.

Rhylan curses. "Stop with your shit, Vik. Why are you here?"

The new arrival looks past Rhylan to us. "For those of you who don't know, I'm Vikarus, Rhylan's twin brother. And you must be the super soldiers that have people in such a spin."

Rhylan takes a sideways step to cut off Vikarus' line of sight and it strikes me as funny that he might be protective of us. "I asked you a question, Vik. Why are you here?"

He shrugs and opens his palms to the side. "Isn't it obvious? I'm here to help you track down your rogue scientist and get back on side with the quadrant."

Lukas snorts. "You expect us to believe you reconsidered and are suddenly Team Thornebane?"

Vikarus rolls his eyes and waves his hand in the air between us. "No. I am and will always be on Team Dragon. Everything I do is for the well-being of my people. It just so happens that the queen wishes for me to make amends."

Rhylan grunts. "How is Mother?"

Vikarus meets Rhylan's gaze, and for just a moment, there is a flash of genuine remorse. "She misses you, Rhy. We both do. We thought you would've come around by now, but you haven't, so we're taking the first step."

"Come around?" Lukas scoffs. "You and your mother sold him out and had him chained to the stocks and sentenced to be whipped to death. If we hadn't rescued him, you would've allowed him to be killed simply for loving Creed."

I exchange wary glances with Link and Shift and then interrupt. "It seems there is a great deal of bad blood spilled between you two, but if I might get back to the point of Andras Brass. Do you genuinely have intel on him or not?"

"Oh, he'll have the intel," Rhylan snaps. "Vik's always had his greedy paws in everyone's dirty business. The problem is trusting him."

Vikarus smirks. "I'm sensing some residual hostility, brother. And, for that reason, I'm going to give you what you want and ask for nothing in return, except perhaps maybe a kind thought in the future."

"Hold your breath until you go blue."

Vikarus chuckles. "You've always been stubborn, brother, but remember, there's a fine line between love and hate. We were once as close as two people could be. We can be that again."

"You're delusional."

He holds his hands out to the side and sighs. "I'm falling on my sword."

Rhylan barks a laugh. "You're playing an angle, the same as always. Now, deliver your message and fly home to Mother to report back like a good little boy."

Vikarus reaches into his pocket and pulls out a small data chip. "This contains the coordinates of Brass's current location. He's been hiding in an underground lab beneath an abandoned factory complex on the outskirts of the city."

"Convenient," Lukas mutters, scowling.

"His defenses are formidable," Vikarus continues. "There are surveillance cameras and motion sensors throughout the facility. Once you advance, he'll know. And the biggest obstacle is the Gen-3 soldiers he has programmed to protect him at all costs."

Link stiffens. "We'll take care of them."

Vikarus shrugs. "You'll find a schematic of the facility, as well as the escape routes."

"And how did you get this information, brother?" Rhylan asks. "Are you in league with him?"

"Well, if not him, then definitely his backers," Lukas says.

"This has nothing to do with you, Lukas. Sleck off and mind your own business."

Rhylan snorts. "You don't give the orders around here anymore, Vik. You gave up that right when you sided with the enemy and joined the rebellion against the Thornebanes."

He shakes his head. "No. *I* honored my duty to my people. It was *you* who sided with the enemy. We were bound to the queen."

"The queen who tried to kill me!"

"Because you were fucking Creed!"

The two brothers meet chest to chest and are about to come to blows when an oversized white wolf and a black bear come racing out of the forest and rush straight to Rhylan.

The two create a united front against Rhylan's twin, and Vik takes a step back. The white wolf rises to stand on her back legs, transforming into Queen Keyla in a graceful motion. The bear, likewise, straightens and stands as Doc beside their mate.

"Hello, Vikarus," Keyla says. "Here to stir up trouble, I see."

Vikarus tips his head from side to side, his muscles tense. "Hello, Keyla. I'd ask how you've been, but I don't care."

"Naturally."

Vikarus looks over the head of our queen and meets his brother's gaze. "You have the intel. I've said what I came to say. You'll need all the help you can get if you want to bring Brass down. I'm offering, but if you don't want me there, I understand. You know how to get in touch with me."

And with that, Vikarus turns and within three running steps, leaps into the air and bursts into his dragon form. A great *whoosh, whoosh,* of leathery wings stirs the air around us for a moment and then he soars into the morning sun.

"Are you all right?" Keyla asks, setting a gentle hand on her mate's arm.

"Yeah. I'm fine."

"Do you believe him?" Lukas asks.

He hesitates, clearly conflicted, before nodding. "Vikarus has always been unpredictable, but yeah, I believe him. We can't afford not to. Whether he's genuine or not, this is an opportunity."

"We can research the intel," I say. "We'll look at it from all angles and decide if it looks legitimate."

"We can never be sure of Vikarus' motives," Lukas says. "But if it serves him and the dragon clans to turn on Brass, the intel could be good."

Rhylan nods. "But we won't learn anything out here. Let's

get back inside and we'll see what we can find out. Between this and Link's program hopefully cutting through the Gen-3 bull-shit, it looks like we're going to have a busy day."

Lark

Standing side by side, Mac and I observe the trainees making their way through the obstacle course for the second day. It's a frenzy of energy, shouts, and the occasional bursts of laughter. From this vantage point, the two of us can monitor their progress and comment on how proud we are of them without them hearing us.

The challenge of training is making them a stronger, tighter unit. It's even better than we hoped.

"They're really gettin' the hang of it," Mac comments, his arms crossed over his chest.

Since Mac has been a soldier for decades, his approval is high praise indeed.

"They're working well together."

"Aye, the kids from the goblin camp and the applicants both. It's good to see them all melding as one unit with a common goal."

"Something like us."

He chuckles and sends me a sideways glance. "Last night was fun."

It was. Even thinking about the food play we shared last night brings a warm glow to my face. It was an erotic deviation from anything I've ever done, but it was so much fun. "I think everyone enjoyed it."

"And by everyone, ye mean Link? Aye, I think he enjoyed it too."

I hope so. "He's trying."

"Aye, I'll give him that."

"Can I ask you something personal?"

He looks at me again and his brow arches. "More personal than havin' my face in yer cunny while gettin' fucked in the ass?"

A tremendous rush of heat hits my cheeks and my core. I swallow and check around us to ensure we still have our privacy. "Well, no. I don't think it's that personal."

Mac is laughing. "I was just teasin', little bird. My point was that if we share the things we do, ye needn't worry about propriety. Ask away."

"You mentioned you spoke with Link."

"That's right."

"And he was with us last night and seemed to have fun sharing our fun."

"Agreed."

"But he and you... well, you never look at him or touch him the way you do with Shift and Flash."

My eyes are drawn to the furthest point of the training ground, where a group of trainees are huddled together, working out a strategy. I'm not sure if I should take closer note of what they're doing, but I really want to finish this conversation.

"Ye see, Link and I talked about that, too. We're not a good fit, he and I. Not like that, anyway."

That hurts my heart. "But he's been struggling... feeling left out. He's starting to understand we're here for him, but I'm worried if he sees your attraction and acceptance to his brothers when he's not welcome, it'll... I don't know. It'll hurt him."

Mac is silent for a moment. "Link is a part of us, just as we are a part of him. The two of us talked about what he wants out of our sexual relationship, and he's only interested in you. He and I aren't attracted to one another like that. And when it comes to Shift and Flash, he's not interested in a sexual foray with his brothers."

"So, where will that leave the two of you?"

"We'll be a team—a family." Mac's hand finds mine, our fingers interlacing in a comfortable squeeze. "Trust me, little bird, all is well. Link has singular tastes and yer the one he wants. As long as he shares and knows he's welcome to watch and parallel play, everyone will be fine."

Yeah. I hope he's right.

CHAPTER NINETEEN

Mac

*a*s the five of us gear up and prepare to leave our suite, I'm waiting for them to address the system fritzing elephant in the room. If I have to, I can do it, but it'll cause more friction coming from me than it will if one of them brings it up.

"Do you think Rhylan's brother would set a trap for us?" Flash asks. "Do people within a family do that to one another?"

I slide my extra ammunition cartridges into my belt slot. "Families have done that and far worse, lad. Relationships are complicated."

It should be Shift. Link and Shift share the calmest report. Or maybe Lark. He seems to consider her words without immediately jumping on the defensive.

"Did his twin really allow people to try to kill him?" Flash asks.

"Aye, on more than one occasion. Vikarus took Rhylan's feelings for Creed as a sign of betrayal. In his twisted logic, he thought he was wronged."

I finish with my weapons check and make eyes at Shift, tilting my head toward Link.

"That's sad," Lark says, strapping on her Kevlar vest. "Rhylan is a good guy. It's not right that he was judged and punished for falling in love."

Shift either doesn't understand my concerns or doesn't want to be the heavy in this fight. Perfect. Even with the three of them on even footing, he and Flash still defer to Link.

"Love is a complicated beast, all right," I say.

When everyone finishes and starts heading to the door, I raise a hand and step into the path. "Seriously, why am I the only one stressed about this?"

Shift frowns. "You're not."

"But ye don't want to bring it up?"

Lark sighs. "You're right. I've been trying to think of a way to say it without it upsetting everyone."

Link stiffens and shakes his head. "Go ahead, then. I'm a big boy. If you're uncomfortable going into a raid with me because you think I'll fail, just say so."

Lark gasps. "No. That's not it. I'm concerned that going into a dangerous situation with your systems faulty puts *you* in danger. I'm concerned about your well-being."

Link chuckles. "But that's not where your concern lies, is it, Mac?"

I lift a shoulder. "Your safety is definitely part of it, but I'm also worried about the safety of everyone else in the raid party. Technically, you are one of the three people least likely to get hurt during an incursion. But Lukas and I are human. The members of Alpha Squad are human. As a commanding officer, it's my duty to ensure my people have the best chance to return home from every mission."

"Link would never endanger your people, Mac," Flash says. "He's the best judge of his status. If he's confident he's fit for the field, I don't doubt him."

I turn to Shift. "What about you, soldier boy? Are you confident in Link's field fitness, too?"

Shift meets my gaze and I see the war waging in those caramel eyes. "Link is self-aware. He has system diagnostics and acceptable ranges of functions. I believe he gets to make his own call on this."

Wrong answer. Raising my palms, I tamp down the fury boiling inside me. "If it makes me the asshole, so be it, but I'm going to voice my concern to Lukas. No one person on a team is worth the lives of the others."

"I'm fine," Link says, his voice hard.

"Right. So fine that ye get up in the night and run the trial centers under the cover of darkness to test yerself to keep the rest of us from knowin'? Yeah, yer fit as a fiddle."

Lark looks genuinely surprised.

Flash looks guilty.

Shift looks pissed. "I didn't realize you saw him."

I shrug. "I'm a very observant guy."

"Do what you must," Link says, pegging me with a dirty look. "If Lukas doesn't want me on the team, I'll stay behind. But with you and your human squad about to face genetically enhanced super soldiers, I'd think leaving one with equal strength and ability home to tend to the hearth would be more detrimental to the safety of your people than me coming—even with the possibility of faulty programming."

Link pushes past me. The shoulder bump is neither subtle nor an accident.

Lark rushes after him.

Shift glares at me and leaves as well.

Flash offers me a sad, puppy dog look and follows along.

I hit the lights and pull the door closed as I leave.

Outstanding. This is a great way to go off to battle.

~

Lark

The journey to Brass's secret lair is quiet and filled with tension. Mac had his moment with Lukas but was overruled in the end. The belief is that having three super soldiers against an unknown number of Gen-3 soldiers is better than two—even if Link isn't functioning at optimum specification.

Mac disagrees, but he's a military man and follows orders. He did, however, make it clear that he would lead Alpha Squad instead of being with us and he wouldn't be responsible for injuries incurred by Link going into battle.

I hate the division.

How did we go from Mac declaring us a unit and a family this morning to this in three hours? The answer is obvious.

Mac is a lifelong soldier.

While I'm a survivor and Flash, Shift, and Link were built to be soldiers, Mac has been in active combat and hostile situations for decades.

He has an unbendable code that he believes in. He lives and dies for his squad. We are supposed to be his squad now, and in his eyes, we let him down.

"Lovely? Are you all right?"

I swipe under my eyes and meet Flash's concern. Of course he came. He feels my emotions so keenly, even when we're not touching each other. "I'll be fine as soon as we end this and get home. We need to make things right with Mac."

Flash scans the empty back lot of the factory we're standing in and frowns. "He was really angry."

"It was more hurt than anger," Shift says, stepping close. "He spoke his truth, and we overlooked his concerns to give Link the benefit of our doubts."

"Were we wrong?" I ask him.

Shift's gaze moves to where Link is perched on the roof of

the warehouse gathering intel. "I hope not, but I don't think we'll know the answer to that until after this mission."

That doesn't make me feel better.

"All right, folks," Lukas says, on the comms. "According to our intel, Brass has an underground lab beneath this abandoned factory. We might find him, his soldiers, an empty lab, or nothing at all. But be ready for anything."

"Especially because the source of the intel is dubious," Rhylan adds. "I don't want any of you killed because my brother thought it would be fun to twist the knife."

"Safe home, everyone," Mac says. "Watch yer backs. Right and tight."

My heart squeezes in my chest and I have to blink fast to stay ahead of the sting in my eyes.

Flash pulls me into his arms. "That was for us. You know that, right?"

"I know."

"That means he's angry, but he still loves us, right?"

I hug him tight and kiss his cheek. "Yeah. That's exactly what it means. And speaking of loving one another, I need you both to take care of yourselves and come out of this whole. I love you both so much."

Flash's smile returns for the first time in hours. "I love you too, lovely. You are my soul."

I meet Flash's lips with a long, slow kiss.

When he eases back, Shift brushes the underside of my chin and steps in close. "Be well, beautiful. Fight hard and if something happens, and we get separated, find Mac. He'll protect you."

I kiss Shift next and my heart aches. Mac should be here with us. They are mates. It must be driving Mac's cat wild to be separated from him at a moment like this.

When I ease back, I see the anguish in his eyes. "I'm sorry he's not here."

"Me too." Shift sets his forehead against mine. "I love you, Lady Lark."

By the time I look up, Link has landed on the graveled ground and is making his way over to us. I can't help but study his gait and the way he's holding his weapon.

Was Mac right to worry?

I know Mac well enough by now to know he wouldn't make a fuss about something or someone just to be cruel or right.

If he's concerned, there are reasons.

"Why do you look so worried?" Link asks, moving into our private little circle. "Is something wrong?"

I hope not. "No. The danger is just settling in. Be careful in there. We've spent enough time at your bedside for a lifetime. Haven't we, boys?"

Shift and Flash both grunt and agree with me.

Gripping both sides of Link's jaw, I pull him down to my lips. Kissing Link doesn't have the sappy passion like kissing Flash or the confident hunger of kissing Shift. Kissing Link is like being the lifeline of someone so hurt and needing that you wonder if you'll ever be enough to heal his wounds.

I don't know if I will... but I'll never stop trying.

When he ends our kiss, we're both breathless. "I love you, Link. It's not always easy, but it's worth it. Be great out there today."

His wink is as cocky and filled with the arrogance I'm growing to find charming instead of annoying. "Why should today differ from any other?"

Mac

From my vantage point on the north entrance, I watch as Lark gives each of them a kiss and they share a private word of encouragement. It's been a fight not to throw my hands into the air and go back, if only to have that shared moment with my mates before battle.

But I'm not wrong.

Still, I wonder what the cost of being right will be. Am I condemning myself to not saying good luck to my people?

Am I torching the foundation I was building with Link because I spoke the truth?

My gran used to say I'm as stubborn as rocks. If it was only about personal opinions, I'd give in. It's not. It's about battle readiness and the safety of the surrounding warriors.

I would never let my pride compromise the safety of the people fighting at my side.

Either Link is too selfish, too inexperienced, or too oblivious to see what he's doing. Because of that, I don't get my pre-battle pep talk or my kisses or my well-wishes.

Instead, I get a twisting root in my gut and a boulder crushing my chest. Lucky me.

"Are we okay, Mac?" Lukas asks, finishing with his weapons check.

"Right as rain, brother. Keep it liquid in there."

Lukas nods. "You too."

The two of us clasp hands and then I'm pulling on my helmet and buckling the snap. "All right, assholes, listen up. In yer weapons, ye've got the finest ammunition Thornebane scientists could make."

"Yeah, baby," Orian says, giving his gun a caress like he's a gowned beauty on a game show.

"The bullets are formulated to take down the Gen-3, but we don't know if it'll have the same effect on Flash, Shift, and Link. I'll thank ye very much to not shoot my mates."

I meet the gazes of the squad assembled in front of me. "Alpha Squad, yer with me. Move out."

CHAPTER TWENTY

Lark

"Super Squad, you are a go." At Lukas' command, Shift, Link, and Flash disappear through the steel door of the dilapidated old factory. *Super Squad*. Flash chose their call sign and man, my guy cracks me up.

I stretch my wings to ease some tension.

It doesn't work.

The building is immense, shrouded in shadows and places for Brass and his Gen-3 army to rig up death traps and places for ambush. Rhylan said there are surveillance cameras throughout the factory, so we assume that now that they're inside, Brass and the Gen-3 know it.

A chill of foreboding runs down my spine.

I push it aside.

As the first female Biome General and Amberloq warrior, I've had to adapt quickly to assume my place, but I'm ready for this.

"Amberloq Team, you are a go."

Dune winks at Lukas and then he, Tundra, and I breach the entrance and begin our tour of the interior.

The insertion is seamless, our approach precise. The murky skylights let in enough light to highlight the basic layout.

It's a long, rectangular building with a tin wall running straight down the center, dividing the space like a long knife cutting through a cake.

With no idea whether the entrance to the laboratory below is on this side or the other, we move deeper to explore.

"Alpha Team, you're a go."

As Lukas gives Mac's group the order to join the fun, I lose focus for a moment and glance around to see if his entrance is on this side of the building.

When no doors open and no one enters, it's clear they're coming in on the other side.

I'm disappointed. I want to see him, even if it's simply from across a dark warehouse. I need to look into his eyes and know we're still a family.

The attack comes quick, and low.

Two hundred and fifty pounds of genetic soldier hits me like a freight train. My wings flare open as I'm thrown sideways and hit the tin wall with a deafening bang.

With my ears still ringing, I widen my stance to keep from falling on my ass. I won't go down. Not unless I have no say in the matter.

As my attacker comes at me again, Dune grabs the guy's arm and slices down hard and fast with his dagger. The guy's wrist detaches from his arm with a sickening crack.

My attacker is fully focused on Dune now and Tundra has joined us, facing off with another Gen-3 we've never seen before.

Damn. How many of these guys are there?

Not that I care. Now that my brain has stopped sloshing in my head, I grab the gun issued to me and get back to the plan.

Find the lab.

Destroy Brass.

Shoot many Gen-3 in the process.

Lifting the aim of my gun, I can't get a clear shot. Both of the Gen-3 are in a tangled melee with Dune and Tundra. The last thing I want is to take down my partners with friendly fire.

Lukas is beside me in the next minute. "Target Dune's first. I'll give you the opening."

He holds up his hands and calls his power. The hair on my arms stands on end and then he fires off a blue bolt of magic. "Dune, down!"

Dune drops without hesitation and Lukas' bolt connects with the Gen-3s shoulder. The hit spins him and offers me an unobstructed target.

I fire two shots in rapid succession, and both are solid shots —shoulder and thigh.

The Gen-3 turns to me in confusion.

Whether his disorientation is because the serum within the bullets is taking hold and shutting him down or he's confused why I didn't aim for center mass, I can't be sure.

"I'm not trying to kill you. We're just here to shut you down." After all, it's not their fault Brass messed with their programming.

Behind us, Dune shoots the attacker going after Tundra. All around us, the warehouse has exploded in the chaos of Gen-3 super soldiers versus our teams.

"We've found the entrance to the underground," Shift says over the comms. "We're entering the lab."

My stomach rolls and I'm thankful I've barely eaten today because if I had a full stomach, I'd be as bad as Yarko right now.

Shift

After finding the access point to the underground lab and notifying the other teams, Flash, Link, and I begin our descent. The warehouse has exploded into a war zone, and it begs the question, if there are that many Gen-3 soldiers up here fighting, how many could there really be down there?

The answer is 'too many'.

Even if it's one, it's too many.

Link leads the way down a rung ladder, but it's not far, so Flash and I just jump. We land in a twenty-foot square room with no obvious exit.

It smells earthy down here, but not unpleasant. It takes a moment to adjust my intake systems. After the booming chaos of the factory, the underground closes in on us with an oppressive silence.

Link tilts his head slightly, as if tuning into some unseen frequency, and then searches for a way out of this room. We were designed for this. Our bio-engineered abilities make us perfect scouts.

And yet, I can't help but worry about him.

Was Mac right?

Flash, always the protector, is tight on his six, our boy's gaze darting from corner to corner, ready and expecting a threat to appear any second.

I sweep my gaze over the far wall, looking for our way into the lab Vikarus told us would be here.

Suddenly, Link holds up a hand, signaling us to stop. His eyes are fixed on a spot in the far corner, where the shadows seem denser.

He strides over, Flash following close behind.

"Wait," I say, rushing forward.

As I reach them, Link is already touching the wall. There's a soft click, and a hidden door swings open, revealing a corridor leading into the darkness.

This is it.

This is where we'll finally find Brass and end this.

The corridor beyond is a narrow chute of darkness, but I see a faint light at the end. Tension coils tight in my gut. The three of us move as one through the silence, a familiar rhythm born of years together in each other's minds.

As we near the end of the corridor, the light grows brighter, and I can make out shapes. A low hum echoes through the space, the eerie symphony of machines at work.

And then we're there, stepping into a cavernous space with a sterile, glass room draped in plastic in the center. Machines are pumping, Gen-3 soldiers are frantically packing, and at the center of it all, like the king of a twisted kingdom, stands Brass.

He must sense us because as we exit the shadows of the corridor, his gaze, cold and unfeeling as steel, meets mine.

A smirk twists his mouth. "Well, if it isn't the Gen-2 triumvirate. I should have dismantled you when I had the chance. Come to put an end to my work, have you?"

"Your work and hopefully you as well," Link says.

Brass laughs. "I heard your enhancements finally presented. It seems my scientists weren't as smart as they thought they were."

"That seems to be a trend with you and your team." I nod to Flash and Link and the three of us fan out, a synchronized move as we prepare for Brass' attack force.

Flash flanks me to the left, his anticipation sparking like live power in the air around him. Link takes the right, the soft glow of his ocular enhancements casting a spectral light on the surrounding machinery.

I move forward, my focus never leaving Brass.

And, exactly as we expect, the moment Brass gives the signal, his forces rush us. I get two shots off, taking down a tattooed female with gills and a man with grass and twigs poking out of his head like hair. They drop to the ground as if I just pulled their plug, which, in a sense, I did.

Flash gets three, his position allowing him a bit more distance and the chance to get an extra shot off.

Link's opponents avoid getting hit and that brings three coming at us from the right, Lion Man included.

The lion charges, a guttural roar ripping from his throat. I meet him head-on, our collision ringing out in the cavernous room.

His strength is immense, but I use his momentum against him, sidestepping at the last second and slamming my elbow into his side.

A battle cry rips through the air. I turn to see Flash tangling with two Gen-3s, their movements a blur of motion. Flash gets off another shot, but the moment one goes down, two more move in to replace him.

Link is engaged in a deadly dance with another Gen-3. His movements are fluid, precise, each strike landing with a precision that soothes my panic.

He's fine. He's holding his own.

Lion Man throws me backward over a steel table and my gimbal system kicks in and keeps my equilibrium stable. I land on one knee and try for a second time to shoot him.

The best part of what the castle scientists did was to genetically tag our DNA to our guns so that no one other than us could fire them. That way, even if we lose our gun in the fight, they can't use it on us.

We learned from their mistake.

Punches land, bones crack, blood is shed. Some ours... and some of the Gen-3s. "This is stupid," I say, evading a roundhouse kick as the alpha lion shoves his boot through the cinderblock wall. "We're brothers. It's Brass who is the real enemy. He's stealing your purpose. He's using you."

As the battle rages on, I glimpse Link out of the corner of my eye. A hard crack to the head has left his steps uneven, his usual grace momentarily eclipsed by the disquieting wobble in his stance.

A chill spears my chest, an icy fear clawing its way up my throat. "Link, watch out!"

My warning comes too late. A Gen-3 fighter seizes the opportunity, lunging forward with blinding speed. He's got a wicked sharp dagger and Link barely pivots in time to keep from being impaled.

He doesn't get away clean though... the Gen-3's attack grazes him and it's enough to knock him off balance, sending him sprawling onto the cold, metal floor.

Flash and I both move to intercept. He's closer and in a heartbeat he's there, placing himself between Link and the Gen-3 as a living shield.

The dagger pierces Flash's throat, and he sinks to the floor, blood coating his neck and chest. Two more join in, the sight of Flash's vulnerability calling them like vultures to a carcass.

There's a harsh, gargled shout, and then Flash is gone, lost to a writhing mass of Gen-3's.

"No!" My voice is drowned out by the discordant symphony of war. Adrenaline roars through my veins, a tidal wave of pure, undiluted fury.

"We need backup. Flash is down!"

I charge forward, my focus on the mass of enemies surrounding Flash. Every punch, every kick, every swipe of my blade extends my fear, my anger, my desperation.

I reach them at the same time Tundra, Dune, and Mac's glorious red cat breaches the corridor.

Mac roars with a vicious snarl, and Flash's attackers move off to defend. During the fight, I lost my gun. Doesn't matter. Grabbing Flash's gun, I slide it into his hand and then aim and fire with my finger over his on the trigger.

Together we take two more downs and then I'm all about my

brother. Calling every ounce of healing energy I possess, I focus on the injuries before me. "Hold on, brother. I've got you."

The world is a blur of motion and chaos. Flash lies on the ground, his eyes wide. Link is bracing himself against the steel table. And now Mac and the others are risking their lives to save ours.

Lark is there next, her pained gasp filling my ears as she drops next to me. "We're here, sweetie. We've got you."

"Finish this!" Brass shouts.

"As you wish, Father." The room spins around me as a familiar voice rings in the air. A shiver runs down my spine, dread seeping into my bones.

I turn and can't quite grasp what I'm seeing.

Beta. Our brother. Our friend. Our ally.

He isn't *ours* anymore.

Beta's focus fixates on me, Flash, and then Link. His gaze is cold and devoid of recognition. It doesn't take much to realize his new directive is to take the three of us out.

With his programming corrupted by Brass's cruel manipulation. He's no longer the Beta we knew.

"Link, you need to keep Beta off me. I need to focus on Flash."

CHAPTER TWENTY-ONE

Link

The world around me has splintered my mind. It is both a cyclone of chaos and a frozen torture. As Shift kneels beside Flash, his hands glowing with a soft, healing light, all I can see is the brutal wound at Flash's throat... the damage his attackers caused to his physical structure... and the vacant stare that tells me his ocular systems are offline.

"Link!" Shift's voice echoes in the chaos, pulling my attention back to him. His eyes meet mine, filled with fear and fury. "Defend us!"

My legs are unsteady, and my systems are erratic. They falter under me, a bitter reminder of my failure.

A failure that's cost us dearly.

Surely there is someone better suited to defend them. Dune and Tundra are working with Lukas and barely holding their own against Lion Man.

Mac has a male pinned by the throat, his cat wild with the frenzy of battle.

Don't they see? Beta is the immediate threat.

Our brother-turned-enemy is closing in on Shift, Flash, and Lark. They need to focus on them.

I push off the table supporting me, but my motor systems don't respond. My legs give out and I try desperately to reroute my primary function to focus on basic functions.

At least if I have control of my body, I can fight.

"Beta, no," Lark says, standing to block him from getting to Shift and Flash. "Fight this. You're our family. This is Brass' doing."

He advances on her.

Defective or not, there's no way I can stand here, hunched over a table while my female faces off against a man ten times her strength and fighting skill.

"Beta, no!" I shout, forcing myself off the table.

He lunges faster than I can move and cracks Lark hard against her cheek. The impact sends her head spinning, her shoulders and hips following as she collapses to the ground beside Flash.

Fury sizzles hot in my veins as I stagger forward. He turns to me, and a bolt of pain sears through my side as he lands a blow. I struggle to stay on my feet, my mind screaming at the betrayal.

He is my friend. I don't want this. But Lark can't withstand his attacks. She is what matters most. I can't lose her. She is mine.

Beta advances again, and I barely have time to dodge his next attack. His movements are fluid, deadly precise, everything we were designed to be.

When his next fist flies at me, I get a block up to save myself from his strike. During the moment we're locked in a hold, I meet his gaze. Nothing of Beta stares back at me.

There is just a cold, ruthless stare of a soldier following

orders. His form towers above me, a monstrous silhouette backlit by the dim lights of the underground lab.

He comes at me again.

His power is incredible, his attacks relentless.

Swallowing hard, I brace myself, my vision flickering so I lose track of the incoming fist. It connects like a concrete wrecking ball to my temple.

He doesn't give me the chance to recover, just lunges forward, a deadly whirlwind of power and rage. I barely side-step his next attack, my systems whirring and clicking as they strain to keep up. I need to push through, to hold out long enough for the others to regroup, to keep Lark safe.

With a grunt, I throw myself at Beta, slamming into him with all the force my failing body can muster. He stumbles, but quickly regains his footing, pushing me away with a strength that sends me sprawling.

I grimace as I push myself up, my systems sending off alarm bells and warning lights. I can't afford to go offline, but it's only a matter of time.

Time that is quickly running out.

I charge again, this time landing a punch that sends Beta reeling. For a moment, I see a flicker of confusion in his eyes. But it's quickly replaced by that chilling emptiness.

I press on, raising my arms, ready to fend off his attack. He hits me again, and it's too much. One by one, in rapid succession, my systems go offline.

Lark

I take the shots needed to drop Beta just as he delivers his final blow to Link, and my surly mate drops to the ground in a pummeled heap.

Beta turns, and for a moment I wonder if he's somehow immune to the serum because he's Gen-1 and it's formulated for Gen-3 but no, after only two staggered steps toward me, he drops to his knees.

And then the room falls still.

Dune and Tundra have finished their battles. Mac is hunched on all fours, breathing heavily, blood dripping from his fangs. And Lukas is helping Shift stabilize Flash on the floor at my feet.

The enemy force is down... all except Brass.

"Where is he?" I ask.

The 'he' is obvious, and everyone looks around. Mac lifts his nose into the air, sniffing, and then his cat lets off a long growl. When he turns tail, I race after him.

There's no way Brass scurries through the cracks and escapes again.

My boots pound heavily on the concrete floor as I follow Mac through a warren of corridors, tracking Brass' scent.

"We're on your six," Dune shouts, not far behind.

Ahead, there's a door hanging open and the brightness of daylight beyond. If he has a vehicle waiting for him, he'll make a run for it.

Mac races through the open door and I'm just behind him. I launch into the air the moment I have clearance to take flight. With my wings pumping, I race over Mac and hurry to keep Brass from reaching a green truck hidden beneath the foliage of two trees.

He's almost to the front bumper.

Taking aim, I fire.

Two shots to the back of his shoulder send him spinning, dropping into the dirt.

I land on a run and grab his shirt, lifting him enough to drive a punch into his face. The crunch of bone is satisfying as hell.

Brass goes limp.

I drop to my knees, gasping for breath as Mac, Dune, and Tundra catch up with me. Dune drops to one knee and checks him before standing and shaking out his wings. "Well done, Lark."

I flop onto the grass on my back and stare up at the sky, trying to catch my breath. "Thanks."

Mac's cat comes over and licks my cheek. His tongue is scratchy and warm. I chuckle and pull him down over my chest so I can ruffle my hands through his glorious red coat. "I love you, puss."

My moment of triumph is short-lived before I hold up my hand and have Tundra pull me to my feet. "Let's get our wounded back to the castle. There's no way we're losing anyone else to this asshole."

~

Shift

I blink my eyes open, and the soft, diffused light of the guest bedroom of our suite greets me. I wince, my head pounding. I try to sit up, but a firm hand pushes me back down.

"Easy, soldier boy. Take it slow." Mac leans forward, brushing a gentle kiss over my lips. "Ye gotta stop doin' this to yerself. It's very hard on me."

"How long?" I ask, my voice raspy and weak.

"Two days." Mac's Scottish accent wraps comfortingly around the words.

I sigh, rubbing a hand over my face. "Flash? Lark? Link? Beta?"

Mac brushes a calloused finger down the side of my cheek, looking sad. "Flash is up and about. He's helping Dune and Tundra set up fer the final trials."

"He is well?"

"Almost back to full capacity. Lark will monitor him, though."

A wave of relief washes over me. "And she's all right? Once the battle ended and we were on the move to save Flash and Link, I lost track of her."

"She had one helluva shiner the past couple of days, but now that you're awake, you can take care of that, I'm sure."

"And Link?"

"His situation was dicier," Mac admits, his brow furrowing. "His system was a mess. But, with the equipment and schematics Brass had in that underground lab, the boffins patched him back together. He's still in recovery, but his systems seem to be stabilized."

"Stable is good. Stable means he's not in immediate danger, but it doesn't tell me if he'll ever be the same."

Mac is silent for a moment, his gaze distant. "All signs point to yes."

"Have they been able to reconnect his communication systems?"

"Some. He's still not on your internal channel, but Josie is hopeful she'll figure that out."

"I hate not having him on our neurochannel."

"The important part is that if something goes wrong, we can step in and sort it out."

"That's a triumph in itself."

Mac nods. "And our triumph over Brass goes well beyond taking him down. With the intel we recovered, we stabilized and reintegrated thirteen of the Gen-3 soldiers into the Amberloq program. We have the information to keep them stable and on-side, and Brass had detailed records of his contributors and their involvement."

"Rhylan must be in his glory."

Mac chuckles. "A happy dragon is a good thing."

I let out a shaky breath. "What about Beta?"

"After a bit of reprogramming, Josie returned his core directives to his designated purpose, and he woke up back to being himself."

"That's a relief."

"So, ye see, all's well that ends well."

I slide my palm across the bedspread and take his hand. "Not quite."

Taking his hand in mine, I consider what I need to say to set things right between us. "I'm sorry I didn't heed your warnings about Link's readiness for battle. Everything you warned us about came to play. He faltered and Flash and Lark were hurt trying to compensate. I honestly thought he could handle it."

Mac purses his lips and sighs. "I was right, but not wholly. Link helped secure the lab. He was a fighting force. There's no way to know if we'd have been able to beat Brass and his army if Link wasn't there."

"So, you're not angry at me anymore?"

Mac shifts to sit on the side of the bed and lifts my hand to press it to my chest. "I was angry, but there will be times when we fire up each other's passions. We won't always agree, and we shouldn't. It's the differences between people that make things interestin'. I love ye, soldier boy. I may have been red in the face furious about lettin' Link fight on yer team, but that was only because I knew who would pay the price if things went badly."

I sit up and lean forward, capturing his lips. "I love you, Connor Mac."

He winks. "What a coincidence. I love ye right back. Now, come along and get dressed. We've got a party to get to."

Lark

Thornebane Castle looms before us, a magnificent structure of gray stone and intricate carvings. The castle grounds are expansive, with lush gardens, towering trees, and cobblestone paths that weave throughout the property. This is where the Amberloq warriors live—and tonight is their rite of passage.

Creed, Keyla, Rhylan, and Doc are seated on their royal dais overseeing the ceremony. Honor, Tundra, Dune, and I stand as the officials of the Amberloq ushering in the new warriors. And Shadow, Lukas and Mac are organizing the trainees, getting them sorted.

"Welcome, Amberloq warriors!" I exclaim, my heart swelling with pride as I look out over the sea of broad smiles. "As warriors, we are dedicated to our rulers, our citizens, and our duty to protect the realm. As we've all experienced over the past months and years, that is not an easy thing."

The kids look up at me, their eyes wide with a mix of emotions—sorrow, determination, but most of all, excitement.

"Today marks the first day of our lives as a united front. You are Amberloq. You represent the best and the bravest of our quadrant. I think I speak for everyone when I say we are honored to call each of you our brothers and sisters in arms."

"Hells yeah, we are!" Dune shouts.

That gets a laugh from the group.

I gesture to the trainees sitting before us, Yarko, River, Bay, Alryx-Ti, and the others. "You survived the trials—in more ways than one—and have risen to meet and exceed everything asked of you in the past weeks. There is more learning to be done, but I know you will tackle it and excel."

I gesture to Link, Flash, Shift, and Beta, sitting to the side of them. "You have been instrumental in our survival and our successes over the past weeks. You have adapted to a world you didn't understand and have stolen more than a few hearts along the way."

Mac snorts. "Not that yer biased on that point."

I chuckle. "I certainly am, and I admit it."

Last, I gesture to the thirteen Gen-3 soldiers sitting to the side. "And to all of you. We got off to an unfortunate start, but you were always meant to be sitting where you are now. You are warriors designed to be the front-line force for the Dornte Quadrant. Tonight, we will toast to new beginnings. Welcome."

They don't seem to know how to respond, so I step back from the podium and hand Honor the microphone. The princess stands at the podium, her long silver hair waving gently in the breeze, her ebony and turquoise wings fluttering behind her shoulders.

"The past two years have been hard. We lost people we loved. Our lives were stripped from us. And the liberties we took for granted were stolen."

I scan the solemn faces of the kids who spent two years with me in the goblin camps. I'm so freaking proud of them I could burst.

"It was a dark time, but we didn't stop fighting. It might've been in biding our time or simply refusing to bow, but we fought to remain who we were."

She twists back to look at her brother, and Creed rises to stand with her. "We fought our way back, we took out the enemies of the quadrant, and even though our forces were decimated, we have now rebuilt our amazing fighting force."

"Amberloq forever!" Dune roars, and the crowd erupts into cheers.

"Amberloq forever!" They shout back in unison.

Creed wraps his arm around his sister and leans forward to speak into the mic. "We thank you for your service. We thank you for moving past what was done to you by the oppressive powers. And we thank you for protecting the Quadrant of Dornte!"

CHAPTER TWENTY-TWO

Lark

Gathered in the rec room of Amberloq Hall, we have a warm fire crackling in the fireplace, the door locked tight, and the drapes pulled closed on the window wall. Haze has been flowing for the past hour, and laughter and a sense of camaraderie pervade the room.

I'm comfy on one of the plush sofas, my head in Link's lap, my feet being gently massaged by a shirtless Flash.

Mac has been regaling us with tales of his younger days, and how he grew up fighting off rogue elements in the streets of Edinburgh.

His animated expressions, complete with dramatic hand gestures, have us all captivated, even as we fight back grins. His stories are always filled with wild exaggerations, but they're told with such fervor that you can't help but get swept away.

Shift is lounging on the sofa opposite us, a relaxed grin on his face as he listens to Mac's tales. Every so often, he interjects with a quip that sends us all into peals of laughter.

It's good to see him give as good as he gets because one of

the first things we learned about Mac is that he's relentless when he's teasing someone he loves.

And he loves us.

Flash, fully recovered from his injuries, was back to brimming with his usual energy almost immediately. He loves Mac's stories and hangs on his every Scottish word.

And then there's Link. My broody boy is quieter than the rest, sitting above me with a soft smile playing on his lips as he fingers through my hair.

Every so often, his gaze meets mine, a silent understanding passing between us. He's still recovering, still adjusting, but he's here with us, and that's more than enough.

As we share the laughter and the lightness in the room, I'm filled with a peaceful warmth. Like Mac said, we are a tight-knit unit—a family.

Our bond has grown stronger, our camaraderie deeper. And as I share this moment with them, I am nothing but grateful.

"All right, enough of the old stories," Mac finally says. "Let's make some new ones." He reaches into the thigh pocket of his pants and comes out with a deck of cards. "I believe I'm owed a rematch."

Shift barks a laugh. "Is that why I caught you putting on two pairs of socks?"

Mac grins. "I've got three pairs of boxers on, too."

The room fills with the sound of laughter and then we're all getting up and moving to the table.

"I wasn't involved in the last game," Link says.

Mac waggles his brows. "Excellent. We've got some fresh blood at the table."

I take another sip of my drink and sit when Flash pulls the chair out for me. "You realize the three of them have super computers for brains, right? The two who are going to be stripping the most will always be you and me."

Mac waggles his brow. "Why do ye think I put on the extra

layers? I want the game to go long enough that we have our fill of strippin' ye down, little bird."

Flash holds out his fist and meets Mac's knuckles in a bump. "I like the way you think, puss."

And with that, we settle in for a night of drunken debauchery with our mates.

And it doesn't get any better than that.

Thank you for reading Trust and Triumph, book three of Lark's trilogy and the last book in the Guardians of the Fae Realms series.
While the story is fresh in your mind, and as a favor to me, please leave a review and tell other readers what you thought. A quick star rating and/or even one sentence can mean so much to readers deciding whether to try a book, series, or a new-to-them author.
Thank you.

If you enjoy my storytelling and want a sneak peek into my next series, turn the page and enjoy the first chapter of Moonstone Maelstrom, a New Orleans Vampire/Witch/Werewolf Why Choose series.

MOONSTONE MAELSTROM
CHAPTER 1

JOSEPHINE

*D*on't freak out. Don't freak out. Don't freak out. Stop freaking out, Josie.

Nope, it's too late.

Sweat slicks my hairline, my heart rate picks up, and the edges of my vision blur. All telltale signs I'm about to hit full-blown freak-out mode in T-Minus—

"Eight... nine... ten." I count quietly under my breath, shutting my eyes against the harsh artificial lights above.

It helps, but not by much. I can still feel the turbulent energy swirling around me in a whirlwind of chaos as crowds of people hustle past in every direction. That is much harder to block out than the glare of a few fluorescent light bulbs, though the artificial light doesn't make the situation any better.

Witches feel things stronger than mere humans. It's part of being in tune with our surroundings, and with Mother Gaia. I've always considered it a kind of sixth sense—an alarm for when shit is about to hit the fan. Except for the fact that it overreacts sometimes, switching into high gear over nothing and causing my entire body to feel like it's going on the fritz.

Like now.

After a sixteen-hour flight from Leeds to Louisiana, I'm exhausted and extra sensitive to the shifting energies around me. It calls to the magic in my cells and ignites against my will before I can do anything to stop it.

The cacophony of dozens of simultaneous conversations fades as my ears *pop* in the same moment the lights overhead flicker. The screens displaying flight departures and arrivals above my head glitches and blinks off, leaving behind a black mirrored reflection, and I watch the confused faces of travelers looking around like they expect to see someone pointing a remote at the screen.

Nope, just Josephine Dumont having a breakdown. Nothing new here, keep it moving.

Breathe.

Inhale through the nose. Hold for two, three, four. Exhale slowly through the mouth and expel the overwhelmed feeling with it. The breathing exercise isn't working, and the anxiety churning in my stomach lurches into my throat, threatening to choke me until I pass out right here in the middle of New Orleans International airport.

"I'm sorry, my computer's gone haywire. What was the name again?" The thick Louisiana accent pulls me out of my mental spiral and brings me some small comfort with its familiarity.

The gate attendant is a small middle-aged woman—her shiny name plate says Lisette—and she leans forward across the little podium desk she's stationed behind, a look of concern etched in the lines of her mouth. "You feeling all right there, *cher*? You're not about to pass out on me, are you? 'Cause you're lookin' awful pale."

The endearment makes tears well up in my current state. Mawmaw is the only one who ever called me *cher*.

It sounds like home.

"I'm fine." Blinking past the sting of unshed tears, I get myself under control and clear my throat.

Now is not the time for crying.

"Claudette Josephine Dumont," I repeat my grandmother's name. "I have all the necessary paperwork here."

I hold out a file folder of pages in shaking hands, but Lisette ignores it and just nods as she flips through a stack of papers of her own before picking up the phone and holding it to her ear. After a moment, she frowns, placing the phone back in its cradle. She tries again, but I'm guessing she still doesn't get a dial tone.

Not surprising–my surge of power took out more than just her computer.

Oops.

"Strange," Lisette mumbles to herself as she hangs up a second time.

She's looking more and more flustered as the seconds drag by. I know the feeling.

"Hold on one more moment, ma'am. We'll get this all sorted and find your grandmother in a jiff," Lisette says.

Sure. My flight landed over two hours ago now. What's another minute or two?

I count to ten and exhale again, focusing on my breathing rather than the torrent of emotions that threaten to make me lose my grip on my magic. Again.

It's been a long day, but it's not this woman's fault I've lost my grandmother and it wouldn't be fair to take out my frustration on her. Lisette is trying her best to help, and I appreciate her efforts. It's more than anyone else has done to rectify the situation. Two other workers have already come and gone in my quest to locate Mawmaw.

She has to be somewhere in this airport. Dead people don't just pop their coffin open for an afternoon stroll. Not even the witchy ones. At least, none that I've seen in the last twenty years assisting Mawmaw at the funeral home she runs—ran—back home. That responsibility is mine now... maybe. I haven't decided if I want to keep or sell it yet.

That's a dilemma for another day.

My life has felt like it's falling apart bit by bit since Mawmaw passed, and it's more than figuring out how to run the business on my own. It's more like having to figure out how to live all over again. Even the basics like remembering to eat or shower.

I don't know what to do with myself now that she's gone.

It's always just been the two of us. Now it's just me.

I wish I had one of the potions Mawmaw was always brewing: luck, nausea, panic, whatever. I would take any of her tinctures right now. One of each, if I could. And a handful of Advil for the wicked migraine I know I'm going to have later. It's already pulsing at the edge of my brain.

The static buzz of a walkie-talkie grates against my eardrums, making me wince in discomfort.

When I look up, Lisette presses the button on the device and speaks into it.

"You're sure?" Her eyes flick to me, and then quickly away again, fixated on the blank screen of her computer monitor instead.

"Did they find her?" I ask eagerly.

By the look on Lisette's face, I'm not sure the news is good, but I still hope.

"Checked and rechecked," the static-muffled voice responds through the walkie, barely intelligible.

Lisette's frown deepens, and my stomach sinks. "I'm terribly sorry, Miss Dumont, but it seems your grandmother's coffin wasn't on the plane to begin with."

That's impossible.

Yet, here I stand without Mawmaw.

"What do you mean she wasn't on the plane? She has to be." My voice is shrill in my own ears, and suddenly I can't breathe, panic bubbling up again and my magic with it.

My fingertips tingle with the buildup of energy, and distantly I recognize I need to keep a lid on my magic before I do something obviously witchy.

Lucky for me, humans like to create their own explanations for the strange and unusual. A bursting lightbulb or a bit of malfunctioning technology barely registers to them these days.

Thank Gaia for that, because the only thing that could make today worse is being burned at the stake.

"I watched the guys on the tarmac loading Mawmaw's casket onto my flight in Leeds. I know she was on the plane with me. It's not like she just got up and walked away."

"Come here, *cher*. Take a seat." Lisette guides me behind her little podium, gently pushing me to sit on a flimsy-looking plastic stool.

I don't realize I'm hyperventilating until she rests a hand between my shoulder blades and urges me to put my head between my knees. After a few gulps of stale airport air, Lisette clears her throat, and I mentally prepare myself for more bad news–though I don't know what could be worse than misplacing an entire person.

If a witch is not laid to rest on their ancestral soil after their body dies, their energy—or what humans might call a soul—can't find rest. Mawmaw will be forced to wander for all eternity, never truly resting.

I wouldn't be able to live with myself if I was responsible for that happening.

"I've had them check the cargo of the plane you came in on, but she's not there."

Lisette presses a Styrofoam cup of water into my hands, and I sip at it while she speaks, focusing on the icy water gliding down my throat.

"They have double checked and triple checked every inch of this airport, but we think your grandmother's casket was misplaced during the layover in Dallas."

"You guys left my grandmother in Texas?"

Being Mawmaw's assistant for years, I've dealt with shipping the deceased overseas a few times before. I have everything I need: death certificate, an official letter from a funeral home. I even have two copies of each, just to be safe.

I have never heard of a body getting lost in transit.

"There is a cargo plane from Dallas arriving in two hours that was on the tarmac at the same time as your layover. We think somehow things got mixed up and the crate containing her casket was loaded onto the wrong airplane."

I stare down at the pages of documents clutched in my hands.

It's like Mawmaw always said: you can't plan for other people's incompetence.

Thinking of Mawmaw hits me with a sharp stab of grief and nostalgia. It's only been two weeks since she passed, and sometimes I forget she's no longer around. I can't just pick up the phone and ask her what to do when something goes wrong.

I have to figure this out for myself.

"I suppose Mawmaw just wanted to go on one last adventure before she's laid to rest."

The tension eases off of Lisette's face and she offers me a sympathetic smile. I think it's more relief that I'm letting her off the hook than anything else. "That's a wonderful way to look at it."

If she knew my grandmother, she would know that I'm not just saying that to make her feel better. Mawmaw was a free spirit—in life, and apparently death, too.

Somehow, I think this is Mawmaw's way of punishing me for doing the exact opposite of what I promised and coming back to New Orleans.

Really, it's her own fault for thinking I would be okay with letting her soul wander, stuck between here and the other side.

I hope you're enjoying one last hurrah, Mawmaw.

"Here," I say, digging into my purse for my wallet. "Can I give you one of my business cards? The number on there is my cell. Will you call me or make a note for the next person on shift to contact me if anything changes?"

"Of course, *cher.*"

The ritual for Mawmaw isn't until tomorrow, anyway. I'll just contact the funeral home in town and explain what happened; I'm sure they'll be more than happy to assist me.

I would do it for one of my clients.

"Thank you for your help," I say before turning on my heel and making a beeline for the exit before my magic detonates like a bomb and blacks out the entire airport.

I step through the sliding doors and into the damp embrace of the humid New Orleans afternoon, so heavy it feels like it's weighing me down. It doesn't help that I'm dressed for Leeds weather, not Louisiana weather.

Back home, we're lucky if the temperature reaches twenty degrees Celsius before June.

Shrugging out of my sweater, I make eye contact with one of the cabbies lined up along the curb just outside the airport, and we share a nod. He snuffs the cigarette out into the sole of his boot before tossing the butt to the asphalt and coming my way to take my suitcase from me.

Sliding into the back seat of the car, I'm hit in the face with a cool blast of air, and I send thanks to whatever life-saving genius invented air conditioning. It's truly a blessing.

"Where ya headed this beauty of a day, ma'am?" The man asks as he slides into the driver's seat, glancing at me in the rearview mirror before putting the car in drive and getting us moving.

Ma'am? Seriously?

"It's Josie," I correct before giving him the address of my hotel.

I'm seriously hoping my room has a nice, deep soaker tub so I can soothe my body and mind with a hot bath. I wonder if there's anywhere nearby I could grab some lavender, or maybe some lemon balm to sprinkle in and keep the nerves at bay.

Hell, after the day I've had, I'll need both *and* a bundle of clary sage.

"Well, how do, Josie? Name's Bernard."

"Nice to meet you, Bernard. You're the first good thing that's happened on my trip so far."

"Aw, you're just sayin' that."

If only he knew.

"You comin' here all the way across the pond and you're going straight to the hotel? No sightseeing along the way?" Bernard *tsks* and shakes his head as we pull to a stop at a red light. "Now that's a cryin' shame. There's too much of this place to see and too much to do to waste a night cooped up in some drab hotel room."

He's right about that.

I've been reading about New Orleans since I was little. Mawmaw never enjoyed talking about it, but that only made me want to know more about it. Growing up, it seemed like a fantasy world.

I have a list of places to visit that's been growing since I was six years old, and only the weekend to check them all off. I'll be lucky if I make it halfway through.

"On second thought, could you take me to Jackson Square? I want to check out the local artists and performers."

If Mawmaw can take a detour, so can I.

"Now we're talkin'." We change lanes suddenly, and Bernard takes the next right, rerouting our drive. "If it's the arts you're interested in, check out St. Louis Cathedral. There's a walking tour that starts there and takes you through the whole French Quarter. You get to see an' hear all about the rich history of the city. Not to mention, the cathedral is practically a piece of art itself."

Honestly, most of the buildings here are masterpieces in their own right. There's so much character in their design.

"Do you mind if I make a call?"

"Not at all. Pretend I'm not here."

I flip through the folder of legal documents and locate the number for the funeral home that's taking care of the USA side of things.

It takes the rest of the ride to explain what happened at the airport, but the man on the other end of the line was more than accommodating. Not only is he going to pick up Mawmaw from the airport, but he's also going to transport her to the cemetery tomorrow.

Which means I have until noon tomorrow to take in the beauty and magic of New Orleans.

"Thanks for the ride, Bernard. And for the chat."

I'm feeling much more at ease now, and eager to explore a bit after driving through it all.

"You're going to love this little city of ours." Bernard pops the trunk open, and I grab my bag. "New Orleans really comes to life when the sun goes down."

Yeah, that's what I'm afraid of.

I've got a good four hours before darkness descends on the city. Plenty of time to do a bit of exploring and grab something to eat before going back to the hotel.

"*Laissez les bon temps rouler*," Bernard says with a wink and a tip of his hat.

Let the good times roll indeed.

I wave him goodbye from the sidewalk and watch the cab merge with the flow of traffic before I turn and take in the glory of Jackson Square.

The plaza is chaotic with people weaving in and out of each other's path. It's much busier than the airport, yet I feel none of the usual anxiety and dread, only excitement and wonder.

It feels right.

It feels like coming home.

Here comes Josephine Dumont ready to take on the Big Easy.

Keep reading: Moonstone Maelstrom

Moonstone Maelstrom:
A Sun Witch Trilogy

It was a mistake I could never undo.

A mistake made with the purest of intentions.

A mistake that locked me in the crosshairs of the most dangerous beasts imaginable—Vampires.

"New Orleans is too dangerous for you, chère."

I thought MawMaw was being protective. Afterall, my parents were killed in a violent car accident in Nola when I was a child. That was when she moved us halfway across the globe.

But a Tremé witch needs to be laid to rest in the soil of our ancestors or she will never be at peace.

The moment I set foot in the city of jazz clubs and soul food, I felt the rush of ancient power. My cells came to life like never before, my connection to the ancestors taking root.

And then he found me—*they* found me. The men of my nightmares. The beasts who capture me and say I belong to them.

Laissez les bon temps rouler.

Don't miss a word of this sexy New Orleans adventure. Click "Read for Free" or "Buy Now" and find out what happens when Emma is confronted with a destiny she can't fight.

Author Note: This is a dark paranormal polyamorous reverse harem series with enemies-to-lovers, fated mates, and band of brothers themes. There will be biting. There will be fighting. And there will be a continuation of the story over the three-book trilogy.

ALSO BY JL MADORE

Find Me

My Direct Sales Site: Shopify

My books

Web page – www.jlmadore.com

Email – jlmadorewrites@gmail.com

Discord— https://discord.gg/uwgngKeF3a

Facebook - facebook.com/JLMadore

Instagram - instagram.com/jlmadorewrites

JL's Reverse Harem Titles

Guardians of the Fae Realms

Guardians of the Phoenix – Calli's Harem

Book 1 – Rise of the Phoenix

Book 2 – Wolf's Soul

Book 3 – Bear's Strength

Book 4 – Hawk's Heart

Book 5 – Jaguar's Passion

Darkness Calls – Keyla's harem

Book 6 – Dark Curse

Book 7 – Dark Soul

Book 8 – Dark Crown

Guardians of the Crown – Honor's Harem

Book 9 – Honor Restored

Book 10 – Honor Guards

Book 11 – Honor Bound

Book 12 – Honor Empowered

Rise of the Amberloq – Lark's Harem

Book 13 – Find the Fallen

Book 14 – Rise from Ruin

Book 15 – Trust and Triumph

Exemplar Hall

Exemplar Hall – Jesse's Harem

Book 1 – Captured by the Magi

Book 2 – Jesse and the Magi Vault

Book 3 – The Makings of a Magi Knight

Book 4 – Clash with the Magi Council

Book 5 – The Unstoppable Storme

Club Sanguine

Book 1 – Moonstone Maelstrom

Book 2 - Sunstone Sacrifice

JL's More Traditional M/F, M/M, or Menage

The Watchers of the Gray Series (Paranormal)

Book 1 – Watcher Untethered – Zander

Book 2 – Watcher Redeemed – Kyrian

Book 3 – Watcher Reborn – Danel

Book 4 – Watcher Divided – Phoenix

Book 5 – Watcher United – Seth

Book 6 – Watcher Compelled – Bo

Book 7 – Watcher Unfeigned – Brennus

Book 8 – Watcher Exposed – Taharqa

The Scourge Survivor Series (Fantasy)

Book 1 – Blaze Ignites

Book 2 – Ursa Unearthed

Book 3 – Torrent of Tears

Book 4 – Blind Spirit

Book 5 – Fate's Journey

Book 6 – Savage Love – epilogue novella

Aliens of Atlantis Series (Sci-Fi)

Book 1 – Taryn's Tiderider

Book 2 – Kai's Captive

Book 3 – Alyandra's Shadow